P9-CRU-189

THE BUZZARD'S NEST

THE BUZZARD'S NEST

Tom West

CHIVERS
THORNDIKE

This Large Print edition is published by BBC Audiobooks Ltd, Bath, England and by Thorndike Press®, Waterville, Maine, USA.

Published in 2004 in the U.K. by arrangement with Golden West Literary Agency.

Published in 2004 in the U.S. by arrangement with Golden West Literary Agency.

U.K. Hardcover ISBN 0–7540–6971–0 (Chivers Large Print)
U.K. Softcover ISBN 0–7540–6972–9 (Camden Large Print)
U.S. Softcover ISBN 0–7862–6545–0 (Nightingale)

The text of this Large Print edition is unabridged.
Other aspects of the book may vary from the original edition.

Set in 16 pt. New Times Roman.

Printed in Great Britain on acid-free paper.

British Library Cataloguing in Publication Data available

Library of Congress Cataloging-in-Publication Data

West, Tom, 1895–
    The buzzards nest / by Tom West.
       p.   cm.
    ISBN 0–7862–6545–0 (lg. print : sc : alk. paper)
    1. Mexican–American Border Region—Fiction. 2. Rio
Grande Region—Fiction. 3. Large type books. I. Title.
PS3545.E8336B89 2004
813'.54—dc22   2004043797

CHAPTER ONE

Seen as the setting sun silvered the broad reaches of the Rio Grande and silhouetted yellowing adobes nestling amid the gray salt brush, there was no prettier sight than Santa Monte. Scarlet strings of peppers dangled from beams, oleanders blossomed in a riot of color, the smooth-topped hills flowed in dun waves beyond. But, at close quarters, the pueblo failed to live up to its promise. Black buzzards preened on the weedy roofs of its crumbling adobes, mangy curs snapped over its offal; the very air was pungent with the foul stench of decay.

Yet its popularity was beyond dispute, for it possessed one outstanding virtue. It lay a stone's throw beyond the law.

Here renegades of every hue found sanctuary. The Rio Grande marked the border, the deadline for warrants and posses. On the south bank of the silty river, they could relax, gamble and guzzle at leisure, thumbing their noses at law-men on the far side of the Rio. And their favorite gathering place was the cantina La Paloma.

At a liquor-stained side table in the decrepit cantina, a gray-skirted rider relaxed, nursing a bottle of lukewarm Mexican beer. He was young, smooth-shaven, with lean features bronzed by the desert sun. In comparison with swarthy vaqueros resplendent in huge black sombreros with tinkling conchas, scarlet sashes, glittering hardware, he was as undistinguished as a gray wolf among peacocks. His dusty corduroy pants were thrust into the tops of high-heeled riding boots, his slack-hanging vest was shabby and the crown of the old Stetson he wore had been punched out of all semblance to shape. Even the butt of the .45 protruding from a worn leather holster, tied down with a rawhide whang, was plain walnut.

There was nothing colorful about Bill Jordan outside of his reputation. Seasoned guests of La Paloma could testify that he was tough as a young range colt and could kick harder. Talk was that he prospered by hazing wet stock across the river, but stepped-up activities of the Texas Rangers had made a sojourn on Mexican soil advisable.

The air in the low-ceilinged cantina was thick with lazy, drifting tobacco smoke, heavy with the stench of sour wine and laden with the rumble of many voices.

Chewing a brown paper quirly, Jordan sipped his beer and lazily surveyed the patrons, bathed in yellow light from oil lamps dangling from the rafters. As usual he sat alone, eyeing all men with an alert wariness, friendly but never familiar. He derived as much entertainment from studying fellow humans as

2

most men did from studying poker hands, and he found it considerably more profitable.

It was a colorful scene, but commonplace to the rider. In the main, Mexicans occupied the tables, swarthy men with flashing white teeth and ready knives. There was always a sprinkling of *Yanquis*—hard-faced *hombres* who wore their guns low; a puncher or two with rope-calloused hands; an occasional citizen at outs with law across the border. A motley crew, laughing, cursing, drinking, wrangling, ready to kill or be killed at the drop of a hat, lurking in a jungle that knew but one law—that of tooth and fang.

Jordan's speculative gaze lit upon a big-shouldered rider, with run-down boots and unshaven jowls, who was slapping greasy cards with three dusky vaqueros at a nearby table. A tangle of dark hair curled from beneath his gray Stetson, and his eyes, with their beetling brows, were a trifle too close set. He'd been around for almost a week now, Jordan knew, drinking hard and drinking alone; he was quarrelsome when he'd absorbed sufficient tequila and plainly on the dodge. Restless, uneasy, a little suspicious of everyone, his demeanor labelled him as plainly as a 'Wanted' dodger. His mouth had a mean twist and there was a slyness in his glance. Slick as calves' slavers, decided Jordan. and a crooked card player. Twice he had slipped out a card, held by a knee against the underside of the table.

Asking for trouble, decided Jordan indifferently. Those sloe-eyed, pocked-faced vaqueros he was crossing were as dangerous as diamond hacks. Give them cause and they'd slash him into hash before he could jerk the gun nestling in his holster. The rider turned his attention elsewhere.

His head pivoted again at sound of dispute from the card table. His eyes narrowed as the big rider's left hand dabbed for the pot, a stack of dingy currency and coin in the center of the table. Sibilant Spanish oaths crackled in angry streams. The stranger half-rose, reaching for his gun. Three knife blades flashed in the lamplight. Simultaneously, Jordan's .45 blared. A vaquero spun around blood flooding his fingers scarlet as he clutched at a shoulder. Jordan thumbed the hammer of his smoking gun. 'Next time I kill!' he announced crisply. 'Vamoose, *amigos*!'

Dark eyes glittering, the two unwounded vaqueros faced the levelled gun. Slowly, sullenly, they slipped their knives back into leather sheaths. One on each side of the wounded man, they eased him toward the dirty fly-curtains that draped the doorway.

It was all over in seconds. No one paid particular attention, although acrid powder smoke stained the murky air. True, the bellowing gun brought abrupt silence, swift side glances from occupants of surrounding tables, but quickly the cascade of rumbling talk boomed out again, and the incident was forgotten. Guns blared and knives flashed with monotonous regularity in the cantina La Paloma. Killings were commonplace; the lazy-flowing river could always take care of a corpse.

Jordan reholstered his gun and took another drink, mentally cursing himself for being an impetuous fool. The stranger had shrunk back onto his chair, momentarily stupefied by the swift eruption of violence. Then he brushed aside scattered cards, swept the stack of dinero into a big palm and dumped it into a pants pocket. Rising, he stepped up to Jordan's table, dropped onto a chair and grinned a trifle shamefacedly. 'Obliged!' he grated. 'The moniker's Smith.'

'You figure on staying above ground,' returned Jordan, with cold disinterest, 'you'll quit tangling with scorpions.'

The other gestured around the crowded cantina. 'Hell,' he growled, with disgust, 'what else is there to tangle with?'

Jordan raised his shoulders and rolled another quirly. The man who called himself Smith called to a hovering waiter. The mestizo, in dirty shirt, flapping white pantalóns and soundless zapatos, slid up.

Eyeing Jordan, Smith inquired, 'What's yours?'

'I got mine!'

Smith eyed the half-empty bottle of beer.

5

'Bellywash!' he grunted. 'Tequila!' he told the waiter, and dropped a silver dollar on the tray.

As the mestizo slouched away, Smith jerked a sack of makings out of a shirt pocket. 'That was sure a lucky shot,' he volunteered. 'I was broke—flat broke.' He patted a pants pocket. 'Now I'm in clover.'

'You hogswiggled the Mex!'

'So what?' returned Smith carelessly. The waiter appeared soundlessly and set a glass before him. He emptied it at a gulp. 'You'd never figure,' he said, 'that I'm worth a quarter-million smackers, gold and greenbacks.'

Jordan made no reply, just sat eyeing the burly, unshaven rider and decided again there was nothing he liked about him. He'd heard many a curious story in the cantina La Paloma. Lonely men, a long way from home, have a habit of spilling their guts to strangers.

'You ain't asking,' continued Smith, fashioning a smoke, 'how come I sold my saddle and eat beans when I own a roll bigger'n a wagon hub.'

'Could be I just ain't interested,' drawled Jordan.

'Not in a quarter-million cartwheels!' scoffed the other. 'You ain't that loco!' He touched a stinker to his cigarette, slumped back against his chair and announced, 'I'm on the dodge!'

'Who ain't?' replied Jordan indifferently.

6

'I'm worth $5,000, bounty money, in Arizona Territory.'

'You're a long way from home,' grunted Jordan, plainly bored.

Maybe the tequila loosened the stranger's tongue, or maybe after hanging around with locked lips for a week he couldn't help spilling words; Jordan didn't know, and didn't give a hoot. He'd decided he had no use for this *hombre,* but that didn't mean he wasn't interested in a quarter-million. Relaxed, half-dozing in the fetid heat of the crowded cantina, he listened while the other droned on, obviously boastful, puffed up by his notoriety, itched by frustrating circumstance.

'Reckon you ain't acquainted with Copper Valley? It lays west of the Black Kaweahs, out in Arizona. Wal, there's four big copper smelters located in the Kaweahs and the payrolls come into Clearwater, the county seat. Every month, regular as the moon changes, they hitch a Wells Fargo Express car onto the local that rolls over the branch line of the Chicago & Rio Grande.'

He picked up his empty glass and yelled 'Waiter!' When the mestizo slid up, he ordered a refill. Glancing across the table at Jordan, he demanded aggrievedly, 'You asleep?'

'Nope,' yawned Jordan. 'I'm too plumb anxious to learn how you latched onto that quarter-million.'

'Easy as slitting a gut!' returned the other

expansively. 'Me and three pards hit the train, blow up the Express car, clean out the dinero and vamoose. I head for my half-section, on Cold Creek, with two gunnysacks chock full of velvet. They weighed plenty! Covering me, Swiveleye stops a slug in the chest. The rat figures he's checking out and spills his guts. A posse comes helling on my trail. We figured to scatter, gather at my place later and divvy up. Wal, the posse pushes me hard. I dump the loot and hit for the Border. Now I got to sweat it out, busted, with two hundred and fifty thousand moldering on my spread in Copper Valley. Ain't that enough to make a man bite hisself?'

But Jordan wasn't paying too much attention. His gaze was directed toward the small square windows that fronted the cantina. Light from the oil lamps streamed through, pooling on the hoof-pocked stretch of ground and ponies tied to the rail He glimpsed two pock-faced vaqueros, sauntering past and glancing swiftly through a window. Knowing vaqueros, he guessed that a payoff was in the offing.

'You ain't through sweating yet,' he replied absently.

'You don't have to tell me,' agreed the fugitive moodily. 'I should be sitting cozy with a quarter-million, and I rot on the River.'

'Could be,' ruminated Jordan, 'your pards got to that dinero.'

'They got nothing, they know nothing!' returned Smith shortly.

'So you cut them out?' inquired the other idly.

'They never was in,' grunted Smith. 'I figured the deal, I grab the jackpot!'

Jordan weighed the train robber with cold gray eyes. This was one hell of a citizen, he thought, a real lone wolf, and crooked as a corkscrew. He should have allowed the vaqueros to carve the *hombre* up. Aloud, he said, 'I reckon you won't be pulling out of Santa Monte.'

'Don't bank on it,' grinned Smith. 'Now I'm heeled, I'll grab me a cayuse and hightail at sunup.'

'Come sunup you'll be floating down the Rio, your carcass ripped from crotch to bellybone,' returned Jordan dryly.

CHAPTER TWO

Smith started at the stark statement. Jordan read swift fear in the renegade's close-set eyes. This *hombre,* he thought contemptuously, was as yellow as a dandelion.

'You stringing me?' demanded the other a trifle shrilly.

'Lamp the windows!' invited Jordan, and sipped his beer.

Smith slewed around, gaze fastened on the fly-specked windows. In the yellow light, the forms of two vaqueros were plain, lounging outside. The features of one were blobbed against a window pane. He stared, focussed their table and pulled back.

Jordan watched Smith as the fugitive nervously fingered his unshaven jaw. 'They figure on knifing me?' queried the other hoarsely.

'You don't doublecross no vaquero—not down here!'

'The law—Rurales?'

Jordan chuckled. 'Law—in Santa Monte?'

Smith's head swivelled, as he scanned the crowded tables, frantically seeking a friendly face where there was no friendliness.

'You got no more chance than a wax cat in hell,' reminded Jordan remorselessly. 'Killings are a dime a dozen on the Rio.'

10

Smith's right hand plunged into a pants pocket. He spilled a fistful of dirty notes and jingling silver on the table. 'It's yours, every dollar,' he ejaculated. 'Just so you ace me out of this tight.'

'Forget it!' returned Jordan with disinterest. 'I don't operate for chicken feed, and I sure ain't wet-nursing no yellerbelly.'

Slowly, the fugitive gathered up his currency and silver, a quaver in his fingers.

Jordan watched with grim amusement. 'Could be,' he decided thoughtfully, 'I'd make a deal.'

'A deal?' Smith eyed him with ill-repressed eagerness.

'Right now, it ain't too healthy for me in Texas. You sign over that half-section in Copper Valley and I ease you outa this tight.'

'My spread!' choked Smith. 'You loco? I got the loot cached there.'

'Wal,' returned Jordan indifferently, 'you sure won't get to spend it.'

Plainly flustered, the other hunched in his chair. The dirty front windows drew his gaze like a magnet, Jordan sat imperturbably, a thread of blue curling upward from his quirly.

'So you figure on gophering around f'r that quarter-million!' exclaimed Smith suddenly.

'If my guess is right,' drawled Jordan, 'there's been plenty gophers already on your half-section, and they located that loot long since.'

11

'Guess again!' threw back Smith sourly. 'Every jasper in Copper Valley, with plows, would never uncover that loot. It'll be there ten, twenty years from now.'

'I'm gambling you won't!' Amusement glimmering in his gray eyes, Jordan nodded toward the windows.

Smith was already staring straight into a pair of vindictive dark eyes, glaring at him through a dusty pane. He looked away, shifting uncomfortably on his chair.

'I settle on that three-twenty acre patch,' continued Jordan matter-of-factly, 'and eager beavers quit poking around. You drift in later, lift the loot and skeedaddle. Now ain't that better'n drifting down the Rio, gutted like a dead fish?'

'Quit dribbling and ace me out of here,' said Smith tightly.

'The price is a half-section,' persisted the other.

'Goddammit, you got a deal!' rasped the renegade.

Jordan nodded. For a while he sat watching the front windows closely. Then, abruptly, he jerked to his feet. 'Dog me!' he snapped.

Smith hurrying at his heels, he threaded between packed tables and headed for the plank bar. Scarce pausing, he threw a few words in Spanish at the squat Mexican bar-keep and dropped a ten dollar gold piece on the wet boards.

By the time he had rounded the end of the bar, Smith pressing behind, the apron had opened a door in the rear wall. Through semi-darkness, they followed his squat form the length of a store room, barrels and stacked cases looming vague on either side. Reaching another door at the far end, the barkeep reached for a bolt. It grated back. The heavy door creaked open and they stepped into pale moonlight. The door slammed shut, and they were left standing on a rough roadway behind the cantina.

'Where you spread your soogans?' inquired Jordan.

'In a stinking adobe, nearby the river,' grunted Smith, fidgeting, uneasy eyes searching the shadows.

Adobes loomed around them, indistinct amid patched brush. Somewhere a guitar tinkled. Nothing moved, but the shadowed quiet seemed laced with menace. Smith jerked back nervously as a bat whirled silently past his head.

'Rattle your hocks!' said Jordan sharply. 'I'll cover you.'

Striding fast, the big-framed renegade moved past darkened adobes, head swerving as he darted quick glances from side to side. But there was no sign of movement and no sound, save the plaintive notes of the distant guitar. Afar off, a coyote pack serenaded the stars with mournful howling.

13

In the rear, Jordan swung around to survey their back trail, etched with shadow. It may have been a trick of the light, but he could have sworn a shadow moved, then steadied. He focussed it, eyes slitted, but Smith was plunging ahead. Jordan hesitated, then followed, not entirely convinced that they had eluded the waiting vaqueros.

Finally, the renegade checked at the sagging door of a crumbling adobe, half-buried in the salt brush on the outskirts of the pueblo. He wrenched the door open and stepped inside. A match flared. He touched it to the wick of a guttered candle stuck in the center of a small table. Jordan stood on the threshold, eyeing the interior by the wavering candle light, repelled by the stale stench that flowed out. He'd seen cleaner pig pens, he registered, noting the litter of cigarette butts and debris strewn over the earth floor, discarded wine bottles tossed into a corner, mussed blankets heaped in another corner. Flies swarmed around the rude table on which stood a greasy plate of beans, half-eaten, a tattered deck of cards and fragments of bread.

Smith dropped onto a bench behind the table with a gusty sigh of relief. 'Wal, we hogswiggled the coyotes!' he grinned, and fished out the makin's.

'Let's just say we got 'em guessing,' returned Jordan. He slapped at a fly. 'Wal—the deed!'

'Hell, I ain't that loco,' threw back Smith

14

carelessly. He thrust into a pants pocket and came out with a handful of coins and crumpled currency, selected a greenback and dropped it on the table. 'Twenty dollars—easy money!'

'Ain't you forgot—we made a deal,' Jordan's voice was soft, almost conciliatory.

'Heck, I was funnin',' returned Smith impatiently. He dropped the currency back into his pocket and with the same motion whipped out his sixgun. The barrel lined on Jordan's chest.

'Grab the greenback and beat it!' grated Smith.

Jordan raised his shoulders. 'If you say so,' he replied resignedly, stepped forward and reached for the creased note.

As he did so, he abruptly and forcefully threw the weight of his body against the table edge. It jammed into Smith's middle. The bench toppled and the renegade spilled backward, off-balance. His gun blared, the sound of the report thundered in the small adobe. Droning high, the slug buried itself in a beam overhead.

Jordan's right foot swung in a swift arc beneath the table. The sharp toe of his riding boot took the falling man low, in the groin. As he hit the floor, he rolled, doubled up with agony. Jordan jumped for him, kicked the gun out of his fist and booted it aside. Then he righted the bench, dropped upon it, jerked his own gun, and sat calmly eyeing the squirming,

15

groaning renegade.

After a while, Smith sat up, retching and clutching his belly.

'On your hind legs!' barked Jordan. There was no conciliation in his voice now.

Breath laboring, the train robber levered to his feet and stood half-bent, glaring at his captor, features distorted with pain and rage.

'So you were funnin'!' mused Jordan. 'Wal, I ain't! If that deed ain't on the table pronto, Mister Smith, you're worm feed.'

'There—ain't—no—deed,' panted the other. 'I—been pitching windies.'

'Too bad!' murmured Jordan. The hammer of the .45 clicked hack. 'See you in hell!'

'Hold it!' gasped Smith.

Eyes baleful, he moved unsteadily toward the pile of mussed blankets. Jordan's cold gaze followed every move. Smith yanked the blankets aside and lifted a warsack concealed beneath them. He fumbled with the tie string of the sack, fingered inside and brought out a folded document. With ill-grace, he shuffled to the table and dropped it in front of Jordan.

'Back—against the wall!' snapped the rider.

When Smith backed away, murder in his eyes, Jordan opened up the crackling folds and scanned the document. It was plainly a deed to 320 acres, located in Copper Valley, Arizona Territory, abutting on Cold Creek and north of Sandy River. But the land was deeded to Jed Harker.

Jordan looked up. 'You Jed Harker?'

The other nodded sullenly.

Jordan found a stub of pencil in a vest pocket, dropped it beside the deed and rose. 'You write this,' he directed, 'across the deed. "For value received I transfer full ownership of this property to Bill Jordan." Maybe it ain't exactly legal, but I guess it's as close as we can get.'

The man who called himself Smith hesitated, scowling at the gun. Then, with an angered growl, he plumped down on the bench and scrawled the words Jordan had dictated, and threw the pencil down with disgust.

Jordan chuckled. 'You forgot to sign,' he reminded, 'and I guess we should have the date.'

When the other had complied, he looked the deed over, stuffed it into a pants pocket and backed toward the doorway. Before crossing the threshold. he paused, eyeing the scowling renegade. 'Listen, Harker,' he said. 'Beat it, right now. Santa Monte never was a healthy spot. For you, it's boothill.'

The other merely snarled.

Jordan rented a room on the second floor of the cantina, approached by a wooden stairway sloping up outside the building. Warily, he ghosted through the shadows back to the center of the settlement. Outside La Paloma a row of ponies stood hipshot at the rail, while from within issued a drone of talk, sprinkled

17

with pungent Spanish oaths. But there was no sign of the vaqueros Smith had hogswiggled. Apparently the pair had grown tired of hanging around. But Jordan, who knew the breed, wasn't fooled.

He mounted the stairway and eased along a darkened passage, doors with daubed numbers opening on either side. When he reached his own room he lifted out his gun, cocked it, threw the door open and jumped quickly to one side. Nothing occurred. Cautiously, he peered inside. Faint in the moonlight that filtered through the cracked window panes were the battered bureau and bed, cradled on raw-hide springs. He slid around the jamb and stood statuelike until he was satisfied the room was empty. Then he closed the door, jammed the only chair under the handle. A man was only careless in Santa Monte once. Relaxed now, he lit a small oil lamp that sat on the bureau and approached the bed to sit down and yank off his boots. Abruptly, he froze, lips tightening. In the center of the frayed quilt, a horn-handled knife was buried, to the hilt. There was no mistaking its grim significance.

CHAPTER THREE

While Dawn was still a promise in the east and cotton-white mist hung heavy over the lazy-moving Rio Grande, Bill Jordan slid out of Santa Monte. Forking a dun as lean and hard-muscled as himself, he eased the pony over the hoof-pocked trail that led down to the river, past silent adobes. Nothing stirred except tethered goats placidly nibbling stunted shrubs and an occasional wandering cur.

Purely out of curiosity, he circled to pass the old adobe where Harker, alias Smith, lived in filth. The door gaped open.

Dismounting, he trailed his reins and glanced inside. Nothing was visible in the gloom. He pulled out a block of stinkers, struck one and peered around. The adobe was empty.

So Smith had vamoosed, he reflected, then glimpsed a Stetson lying amid the debris that cluttered the hard-packed earth floor. He quickly stepped inside and touched the dying match to the stub of candle bedded in grease on the table.

Blankets were still heaped in a corner. He bent, fingered them and felt dampness. In the pallid candle light he eyed his fingers. They were reddened and sticky.

So the vaqueros found Smith! That shadow

19

had moved last night. Well, the carcass of many a better man had drifted down the Rio Grande, he considered philosophically, and headed for the crossing.

* * *

Forking a hock-scarred dun, a gray-shirted rider beat across the glaring flats of a broad valley. Away to his left, drooping willows marked the looping course of a stream. Eastward, the desolate flanks of a mountain range gleamed black, blotched with yellow. Spirals of greasy smoke twisted skyward, drifting across barren benches like noisome fog. That would be the Black Kaweahs, reflected the rider, and the smoke marked smelters. The gent who called himself Smith hadn't lied so far.

On the opposite side of the valley, bulking against the western horizon, the vulcanic walls of another somber range swept up, flattening into plateaus, climbing to craggy heights, topped by dark spurs, etched stark against the blue.

The verdant ribbon that marked the course of the stream curved across his front. The pony dropped down the sandy slope of a collapsed cutbank and stood hock-deep in a still pool, covered by a glittering dust film. This must be Sandy River, considered the rider, as the pony blew through dirt-encrusted

20

nostrils and nuzzled the water. Here, as it flowed into the desert, the water course had shrunk to a succession of drying waterholes, before it was finally swallowed by the ever-thirsty sands.

Jordan built himself a smoke and again lifted his reins. Dust rose to form a skin-prickling aura around horse and rider, as the dun began to jog northward again, but the gray flats, seamed by green threads of chaparral—greasewood, sage, maguey—made pleasant contrast to the alkali sinks, eroded rock escarpments and the baked clay of the desert they had left behind.

In the distance, the rider sighted cows, drifting in long files toward water. The metal blades of a windmill, protruding above the rounded shoulder of a hill, heliographed bright flashes as it slowly whirled. The distant high-pitched note of an engine whistle pricked through the purple heat haze.

As the sun climbed higher, and the rider worked up the valley, outlines of buildings bulged against the horizon. Pulling closer, Jordan heard the crash of shunting cattle cars, the rumbling complaint of penned steers, the shrill yells of herding punchers.

He jogged past dust-veiled cattle pens, a paint-peeling railway depot, and found himself on a wide, sandy stretch of street, and reined down to a walk.

So this was Clearwater! He jerked the dust-laden brim of his Stetson lower and gazed around with interest. A sprinkling of shirt-sleeved citizens moved sluggishly along gritty plankwalks, shaded by wooden canopies projecting from square-fronted stores. Here and there a pony at the hitchrails flicked flies. The horses were thickest outside an ugly clapboard structure, whose sign proclaimed it to be the Maverick Saloon.

The rider's gaze flicked over the striped pole of a barber shop, a sprawling general merchandise store and a long building with faded canvas awnings, labelled Clearwater Hotel. Straw-hatted Mexicans lazed in shady alleys; a row of punchers, with sun-blackened features, hunkered imperturbably against the saloon front; two bonneted women chatted in a store entrance.

Cross streets gave glimpses of weary frame buildings, grateful for the shade of fluffing cottonwoods. Then, as his mount drifted ahead, Jordan's searching eyes lit on a square, red-brick building, set back from the street and fronted by a broad flight of brick steps. Its windows were tall and narrow and a design picked out in the brickwork made the words CAMAS COUNTY COURTHOUSE.

He neckreined the dun to the rail outside the courthouse and swung stiffly to the ground, saddlesore from long hours on the trail. Climbing the steps, he pushed back a glass-panelled door and found himself in a wide, gloomy corridor. Spur chains jingling loud in the quiet, he paced past solid oak doors, a neatly lettered inscription across the panel of each—County Auditor, Tax Collector, Courtroom. At Recorder he paused, eased the door open and entered.

A mousy little man slipped off a high stool and eyed him expectantly through a wicket.

'I bought a half-section north of Sandy River,' drawled Jordan. 'Figured I should record it.' He fished out the deed Harker, alias Smith, had signed over and pushed it through the wicket.

The clerk removed a pair of steel-rimmed spectacles, polished the thick lenses carefully with a slip of blotting paper, picked up the deed and examined it. Watching, Jordan saw him start. His hcad jcrkcd up and he shot a startled glance at his visitor. 'This,' he said accusingly, 'is Jed Harker's holding!'

'What of it?' inquired Jordan carelessly.

'Harker's a criminal, a wanted man.'

'I didn't ask for references,' Jordan threw back, offhand. 'Just bought thc land, and paid for it,'

Plainly in a quandary, the clerk again peered at the deed, then, with muttered apologies, darted out of sight behind shelved file cases.

Jordan was placidly smoking when he returned, visibly excited. 'This—er—transfer, Mr.—'

'Jordan!'

'Mr. Jordan, is most irregular. Possibly it is legal. In any event I must consult an—er—authority, and retain the deed.' He scribbled on a sheet of paper and pushed it through the wicket. 'Your receipt!'

Stalling, thought Jordan. Well, they could quibble about legal ownership all they wanted. All he needed was to establish a claim that would enable him to squat on Harker's half-section and poke around. 'Suits me!' he shrugged, jammed the receipt into a vest pocket and moved toward the doorway.

As he stepped out into the corridor, two waiting deputies closed in on either side.

If Jordan was surprised, he gave no indication of the fact. He checked, looking from one to the other with faint amusement.

'Sheriff Haslipp wants you!' barked the foremost, a hard-eyed, leathery-featured man.

'For what?' inquired Jordan guilelessly.

Without bothering to answer, the leathery-faced deputy dropped a hand forcibly upon the rider's shoulder. Jordan jerked free and his right hand dropped to his gun butt. Faster than a snake strikes he whipped the gun out. Before either deputy could grab for his own iron, Jordan covered them.

'Freeze!' he barked, eyes hard as twin bullets. 'Next time you clap your grubhooks on me, lacking a warrant,' he told the leathery-faced deputy bleakly, 'I'll feed you a pill you

24

sure won't digest.'

'Now feller, there's no call to get your bristles up,' put in the other deputy placatingly. His pard had backed a pace, wary eyes on Jordan, hand inching toward his own gun butt.

'Just so you don't prod,' returned Jordan. 'Wal, just where do I find this sheriff?'

The friendly deputy, a stringy fellow with a whimsical twist to his lips, nodded down the corridor.

Jordan holstered his gun and strode past them. He could hear the two pacing bchind. At a door inscribed County Sheriff he paused momentarily, then entered.

At the further end of a high-ceilinged room a man past middle age was seated at a battered roll-top desk, a long, black cigar between his lips. A sheriff's badge was pinned to his blue shirt and his dark pants were stuffed into knee boots. Weighing him, Jordan's quick glance took in the graying mustache curved over firm lips, the belly bulging over his belt, the eyes deep set in desert-eroded features, reflecting weary patience. A shrewd old law hound, decided the rider, but he'd reached the age where a swivel chair was a heap more controllable than a saddle.

Rows of 'Wanted' notices plastered the walls, against which several straightback chairs were lined. In a corner stood a gunrack, holding sawed-off shotguns.

25

The two deputies came into the room behind him. 'The hairpin's techy as a teased snake,' announced the leathery-faced man, talking to the sheriff, past Jordan. 'The bustard pulled a gun on us.'

'Forget it, Pecos!' smiled the sheriff. To Jordan he said amiably, 'Rest your legs!'

The rider dropped onto a chair beside the desk, and noticed that his deed lay before the lawman.

'You claim you—bought this land?' queried Haslipp.

'Sure!' threw back Jordan. 'Any objections?'

The sheriff drew slowly on his cigar, eyeing his visitor. 'Just can't figure why he'd sell.'

'Could be he was short of dinero.'

'You didn't know Harker was a fugitive, from a murder warrant?'

'Should I have known?' The sheriff ignored the irony in Jordan's voice.

'And that he cached a quarter-million, in gold and currency, on that spread?'

'Seems I made a good buy,' commented Jordan, with a slow smile.

'Quit sidestepping!' Haslipp's voice hardened. 'Could be you're working in cahoots with Harker.'

'He just ain't my type,' drawled the rider.

'Where did you meet up with the coyote?'

'On the Rio Grande, Texas way.'

'And where would he be right now?'

'Your guess is as good as mine, Sheriff.'

26

Jordan turned and eyed the leathery-faced deputy, who was carefully scanning the rows of pin-ups. 'You won't find me there!' he said offhand.

'Don't bank on it,' growled the other.

'Now listen, Jordan,' put in the sheriff, sharply. 'Maybe you're as dumb as you act, but I doubt it. My guess is that Harker made a deal with you to dig up the loot, meet him over the border, and split.'

'You sure misread my brand, Sheriff,' protested the rider.

'Could be,' agreed the lawman, 'but don't ever forget this—the moment you finger that loot you become an accessory. The charge is train hold-up and murder. That means the rope!'

'This is sure one hell of a greeting for an honest citizen!'

'But,' went on the sheriff, 'if you should locate the loot—by accident'—Jordan heard a snort from Pecos, behind him—'Wells Fargo has a standing reward for return of the dinero-20%. Lead us to Harker and you collect $5,000. There's $1,000 apiece for arrest and conviction of his two accomplices.'

'I could wallow in velvet!' returned the rider blandly. He rose, 'Wal, can I beat it?'

'We got no reason to hold you—yet,' retorted Haslipp dryly. 'I could give you a slice of parting advice,' he added thoughtfully.

'I'm sure all ears!' smiled Jordan.

27

'Stay away from Harker's spread.'

The rider's brow creased. 'Hell, I own it!'

Haslipp raised his shoulders, 'Mebbe so, but the day you take possession you sure as hell sign your own death warrant.' He turned to his desk, 'So long! It's your funeral.'

CHAPTER FOUR

For a long moment Jordan stood eyeing the sheriff's broad back, wondering just what grounds the lawman had to justify the ominous prophecy. A chuckle from Pecos brought his head around to survey the hard-faced deputy. The other deputy, too, seemed to be amused. They must sure figure he scared easy, considered the rider, and headed for the doorway.

At the top of the courthouse steps he paused in the shaded entrance, absently making a cigarette and reflecting upon his next move. The sheriff's dire warning that death lurked on Harker's spread was already fading from his mind. Some *hombres* had a queer sense of humor.

As his fingers fashioned the smoke his eyes dwelt on the sleeping street. The sun was beginning to drop westward and the shadows were inching across the ruts. Life stirred sluggishly—a pack of mongrels snarled around the mouth of an alley; two dawdling boys plowed side by side through the ankle-deep dust, deliberately stirring a fog; a knot of little girls clustered at a store window, chittering like sparrows. School must have just been let out, he decided. Then his attention quickened as he focussed on a girl, dark-skirted, with a white shirtwaist, stepping briskly along the plankwalk, approaching the courthouse. Something about her mien, the uplift of her small chin, the swinging freedom of her stride, the grace of her lithe figure held him. From the crown of her head to the soles of her neat shoes she seemed to exude a joyous vitality.

As she passed below him, unaware of his presence beneath the shaded doorway, he could hear her humming a gay tune. His glance dwelt upon oval features, sun tanned and crowned by a glory of dark-brown hair. A bonnet swung carelessly from one hand, while the other arm was crooked, nursing a number of books.

Young, he thought, and carefree as a colt. He'd gamble she hadn't seen twenty yet. The gal was sure a sight for sore eyes. Oblivious of his scrutiny, she passed the steps.

The yapping of the mongrel pack suddenly gained in volume. Strung out, they angled toward him, in frantic pursuit of a mangy yellow hound whose desperate flight was slowed by a huge chunk of raw meat clutched in his slavering jaws.

Amid a discordant yapping chorus, they swept over the plankwalk and shot past, in the wake of the lissome girl. Overtaken by several snapping curs, the yellow hound leaped ahead in blind panic. The half-made cigarette dropped from Jordan's fingers. He opened his mouth, but before he could yell a warning, the yellow hound plunged between the girl's legs, became enveloped in her skirt. In an instant she was swept off her feet and had thudded on to the planks with a muffled scream. The books were scattered pell-mell and her prone form seemed instantly to be smothered by a flurry of snarling curs.

Jordan tornadoed down the steps and bounded into the melee. Vigorously booting off yelping dogs, he bent, grabbed the victim around the waist and set her on her feet. Another mongrel had snatched the coveted chunk of meat, and dashed away. The pack followed in full cry.

Jordan stood anxiously eyeing the dishevelled girl. Her white shirtwaist was now dust-smudged, her dark skirt gray with grime and her hair awry. He expected tears and hysteria but her level brown eyes reflected nothing more than bewilderment, and her red lips twisted with amusement rather than fear.

'Well,' she said, 'anything can happen in Clearwater!'

'You hurt any?' he demanded.

She smiled and the dusty smudges on her cheeks seemed to impart an added piquancy to her features. 'My feelings are lacerated,' she admitted cheerfully. 'I must look like a scarecrow.' She ruefully eyed her mussed clothing and began beating the dust off her skirt. Jordan busied himself gathering books.

When he straightened, she had patted her hair into place and repaired much of her dishevelled appearance. There was warmth in the glance she directed at him. 'I haven't thanked you yet, Mr.—'

'Jordan!' he supplied. 'Bill Jordan.'

'I'm Carol Hall; I teach school.' She extended her hands for the books.

'Guess I'll side you down street aways,' he decided. 'Them doggone mutts are still running wild.'

She smiled acquiescence and he dropped in beside her, still packing the books.

'You must be a stranger in town, Mr. Jordan,' she commented. 'I'm acquainted with most everyone around here.'

'Just rode up from the Rio Grande,' he said offhand, 'taking over Harker's spread.'

'Jed Harker!' With the exclamation, she jerked to a stop, swinging around to face him.

'Sure!' he agreed, poker-faced.

'Harker's a killer, and a fugitive.'

Jordan shrugged.

She stood eyeing him levelly. Then, with tight lips, she turned away. As they moved along the plankwalk again, Jordan sensed a subtle change in her demeanor. The friendliness had evaporated.

'Listen!' he expostulated. 'Harker's no pard of mine. Our trails crossed on the Rio Grande, He had a half-section to peddle, I made a dicker.'

32

'For a share in the train loot he left behind,' she retorted, her voice tight.

'Loot?' he returned blankly.

'Mr. Jordan,' she said coldly. 'I am not a fool. In the first place, Harker wouldn't sell his half-section, not with a quarter-million loot buried somewhere on it. In the second place don't expect me to believe that you bought a ranch you'd never seen, in country you were unacquainted with, unless there was a very special inducement.'

'The price was right!' he returned defensively.

'I can imagine that!' she threw back. 'How much did Jed Harker cut you in for?'

He said nothing. Again they walked in silence. Then the girl spoke again, less heatedly now. 'I'm sorry if I am misjudging you, Mr. Jordan, but I have a personal reason to detest that renegade gang. Tom Furness, the Express company clerk Harker murdered, was my cousin. He left a widow and two children.'

Again Jordan made no reply. There seemed to be nothing he could say. The plankwalk came to an end at a side street. The girl stopped and reached for the books. 'Thank you!' she said impersonally. 'My boarding house is just a few steps down this street.'

Without comment, he handed her the books. It was plain that this spirited young school ma'am had no use for any associate of

33

Jed Harker. He was about to turn away when her voice checked him. 'Mr. Jordan! There are strange tales floating around regarding Harker's place. Folks claim there is a curse on the ranch and sure death awaits anyone who spends a night in the cabin. Even the cowhands ride around it.'

'I don't scare that easy, ma'am,' he returned with amusement.

'I am simply warning you,' she replied shortly.

'Could be the Valley folks just hate to think some stranger might light on that loot.'

'It could be true!'

'Guess I can take care of myself,' he retorted, a trifle grimly.

'I hope so!' she threw back and swung away.

Jordan stood watching her trim form as she picked a path around the potholes of the side street. There seemed to be a conspiracy in Clearwater to scare strangers away from the train robber's spread.

He sauntered back to the tie rail outside the courthouse, loosed the dun and mounted. At a walk, he hit for the Mercantile Store down the street.

Inside the store, he pushed a pencilled list he had made out the previous evening across the counter. The storekeeper, a grizzled oldtimer, bustled around, gathering a growing stack—airtights, bacon, coffee, flour, beans. The pile complete, he began stowing it in a gunnysack.

'Prospector?' he inquired casually.

'Rancher!' replied Jordan. 'I'm taking over Harker's place.'

The storekeeper shot him a quick glance, opened his mouth to speak, changed his mind and picked up the twenty-dollar gold piece his customer dropped on the counter.

'You were saying,' prompted Jordan, with inward amusement. Another warning, he thought.

'Just thinking,' replied the other soberly, 'what a dang pity to lose a cash customer.'

'Heck, I'll be back.'

The grizzled man shook his head. 'You'll be brought back, and planted in boothill. Two gents have squatted on Harker's place since that coyote lit out. Both were found dead.'

'Seared to death?' inquired Jordan gravely.

'Nope—shot!' returned the storekeeper shortly. 'Both stopped a .44 slug—high and center.'

'Any arrests?'

'Arrest!' snorted the other. 'Arrest who?'

Outside, Jordan secured the bulging gunnysack behind the cantle and headed up Main Street. The storekeeper had told him that Harker's place lay about twenty miles north, on Cold Creek, bordering Sandy River. And the old man had acted like he was chief mourner at a funeral.

Through lengthening shadows, the dun

35

jogged along a trail that wound beside the stream. At sundown, Jordan made camp among spreading willows on the river bank. Supper over, he hunkered beside a small fire, sucked a quirly and soaked in the peace of a tranquil evening. Nearby, his pony cropped peacefully. The river whispered past, its placid surface fretted with widening rings as fish rose for the gnats. Rabbits rustled through the brush, flirting their white tails. Blue jays chattered among the branches, a dove cooed melodiously downstream. Thought of the school ma'am drifted into the rider's mind. A looker, he mused, and spirited, too. He'd gamble she'd soon be running in double harness. Chances were she had a dozen suitors dangling right now. Somehow the idea of Carol Hall married didn't give him much pleasure.

Then he fell to musing on the curse that it was claimed rested on Harker's place. The sheriff and the storekeeper might have been hurrahing him, but he'd swear the girl was in dead earnest. Two dead men! That didn't sound good. The point was—did they exist except in the storekeeper's imagination. Could be the Valley folk just craved to scare strangers away. If anyone turned up that loot they wanted it should be one of their own. Satisfied, he rose, scattered the embers of his fire and spread his soogans.

The rising sun had not yet cleared the rugged silhouette of the Black Kaweahs when he was again following the curves of the river. The current ran faster now and the terrain slanted upward as the dun plugged toward the rim of the valley. Jordan began to give more attention to his surroundings. Harker's layout should lie somewhere around.

He focussed a cabin, pole corral and shanty barn to one side, standing nearby a mott of scrub oak, a half-mile or more from the river bank. Between cabin and stream lay a grassy flat, and just beyond the buildings a winding thread of green marked the snaking course of a creek. Beyond, low hills rolled in gentle undulations, swelling higher and higher, until they finally merged into a ragged malpais of upended terrain, riven by gulches, scabbed by boulders and clothed with scrub brush.

Angling away from the river, Jordan headed for the cabin. It was plainly deserted. The door gaped open, the stovepipe chimney leaned drunkenly. Weeds grew thick in the corral. Over all hung an atmosphere of desolation.

But Jordan had once been a cowman and he noted with satisfaction that there was ample water and graze aplenty. And that graze sure wasn't going to waste, he concluded, noting the cows bunched thick across the flat and standing in the shade of scattered scrub oak. They all carried the same stamp brand—a turtle.

Outside the cabin, he swung out of leather. Dumping the sack of chow on a rude bench, he made a leisurely survey of his surroundings. Signs of neglect were everywhere, but what took his eye was a checkerboard of shallow excavations that pitted the ground. He considered them with a puzzled frown, until the explanation entered his mind. Treasure hunters had been busy, systematically digging.

Shrill yippees, the rumbled protest of cows and splashing from the direction of the river drew his attention. Two riders were hazing a big bunch of stock across stream. Crowding more cows onto Harker's graze he thought. These Turtle critters were swamping it already. He planned to run a few head himself, for sake of appearances. Before he could do so, these strange cows would have to be pushed back across the river, which was apparently where they belonged. Well, now was as good a time as any.

He mounted, lifted his coiled rope off the strap and began to round up the stock on the flat, swinging a loose rope's end. He was hazing a goodly hunch toward the river when the two riders became aware of his intent. One on the further bank and the other sitting his pony, belly-deep in mid-stream, they watched with apparent bewilderment. Then, with a yell, the rider on the bank headed into the stream. Water cascading, he urged his mount across. His pard joined him. Water streaming from their ponies, they breasted the nearer bank and spurred toward Jordan.

CHAPTER FIVE

Jordan reined up when the two punchers yanked their ponies to a halt a dozen paces distant. Hands resting upon his hips, he sat eyeing them coolly. The foremost was a squat, muscular fellow, dark hair curling from beneath a battered Stetson. An overshot jaw and misshapen nose gave him a truculant appearance, intensified by a jagged knife scar that etched his forehead. He wore his gun low, Jordan noted, with a flared holster to facilitate a fast draw. His pard, a squat saddleworn rider, with patched levis, displayed less belligerence, reining back a mite.

'You hunting trouble, mister?' rasped the scarred rider.

'Nope,' Jordan told him mildly, 'just clearing my range.'

The other spat. 'Your range! This is Harker's place, and Harker's on the lam.'

'I bought it!'

'You're a cockeyed liar!' derided the other. 'Anyways, the Turtle needs the grass and the Turtle's gonna use the grass.' Across a shoulder he barked, 'Push what's left of them steers across, Baldy!'

'Hold it!' snapped Jordan.

The squatty puncher sat his saddle uneasily, glance darting from one belligerent to the

39

other. His pard's right hand dropped negligently over his holster. 'Hop to it, Baldy!' he growled.

'You move just one more cow critter onto my range and I'll drop you,' promised Jordan pleasantly.

The scarred man's eyes glinted with cold satisfaction. 'You asked for it, mister, and you're gonna get it,' he grated. His rope-scarred hand closed on the butt of the holstered .45. He jerked the weapon out of leather.

As the gun arced down and he thumbed the hammer, Jordan's gun hand blurred down. His Colt stabbed flame.

The impact of the slug twirled the scar-faced puncher half around, almost unseating him. His gun thudded to the ground, released by paralyzed fingers. A fast-spreading red patch stained his right shoulder. Mouth agape from shock and surprise, he stared at Jordan as though stupified, clutching the smashed shoulder with his left hand.

Smoking gun levelled, the new owner of Harker's place eyed the puncher called Baldy. 'Crave to take it up?' he inquired, an edge to his voice.

'No siree!' declared the squat rider. 'Sudden there fancies hisself with a smoke-pole. Me, I'm just a cow nurse.'

'Then haze them Turtle cows back across river,' directed Jordan. 'Every doggone steer!

40

In future, stick to your own side of the stream.'

'Sure!' agreed Baldy hastily, wheeled his mount and pricked it into a lope.

Jordan built a smoke and slacked in the saddle, watching the Turtle puncher gather the stock spread across the flat and push it toward the river. Nearby, the wounded rider had slid out of leather and was clumsily stuffing his bandana inside the blood-soaked shirt.

This Baldy was a fast man with stock, decided Jordan, as the Turtle puncher completed his chore and headed back. The flat was clear and steers bunched across stream, lowing protest.

When the stocky rider jogged up, Jordan nodded in the direction of the wounded man, who slacked against his mount, clutching the horn for support.

'Better get that gent to town and have the sawbones fix him up,' said Jordan.

The two drifted over to the crippled puncher. 'Buck'll nail your hide to the barn f'r this,' he declared thickly, glowering at Jordan.

'And who might Buck be?' inquired Jordan, with cold disinterest.

'Buck Burdock's the boss,' supplied Baldy. 'Rods the Turtle, ranges most all the upper valley.'

'And craves more!' commented Jordan. 'Wal, beat it!'

The squat puncher boosted his pard into the saddle and the pair splashed across stream.

Jordan watched as their mounts jogged across the swales, growing steadily smaller with distance. Finally, when they were no more than dots dancing through the heat haze, he lifted his reins and headed back to the cabin.

When he stepped through the open doorway, straddling a trench excavated the length of the threshold, he checked with a low whistle of disgust. It was apparent that the treasure hunters had not confined their efforts to digging outside. The square cabin was crudely furnished. A wooden bunk had been built at one end. In the center stood a rough table and at the other end a small sheet iron stove and wood box. Above the stove, two shelves ran the width of the cabin. Beneath them, a few cooking utensils hung from spikes.

The floor was packed earth, with a border of adobe-like bricks set around the stove. Many of the bricks had been wrenched out of the ground, probably with a pick, and were scattered around. On the bunk, a dingy mattress was ripped along its length and cottony fluff billowed out. Knocked down, the stovepipe lay in lengths on the floor, spilling soot. Cans and dishes had been swept off the shelves and lay around in disorder. In one corner, a hole had even been dug in the floor. Knee-deep, it gaped black, fringed with mounds of crumbly earth. Everything, from the stable lamp suspended from a hook in the ceiling to articles of clothing dangling from pegs, was coated with mingled soot and grime.

Jordan sighed at thought of the clean-up that lay ahead.

He retreated outside, led the dun to the weed-grown corral and stripped off its gear. Then he investigated the interior of the barn and found more evidence of digging. Two buckets, a shovel and other implements were heaped in a corner. He picked up the buckets, found them sound, and followed a well-worn path down to the creek, a few paces beyond the rear of the barn. Brush grew thick along the cutbanks of the creek and was already invading the path. Pushing through, he slid down a slope and filled his buckets. One he set inside the pole gate of the corral for his pony, the other he packed back to the cabin. Unbuckling his gun-belt and peeling off his shirt, he began the cleaning chore.

He dumped the ripped mattress, fixed the stovepipe, reset the bricks and filled the hole in the floor. In an hour the place began to look livable. He was washing off the shelves when the faint click of a shod hoof upon rock reached his ears. In a flash, he jumped for his gunbelt and swung it around his middle.

Buckling the belt, he eased up to the open doorway, peering out. A rider was approaching, astride a calico pony, riding bareback. The stranger was clad in a flaming red shirt and dirt-slick levis. His features were swarthy and cheeks high-boned. Moccasins

43

encased his dangling feet and a wide brimmed sombrero crowned a shock of rusty-red hair. Jordan's probing scrutiny revealed that the newcomer wore no gunbelt, but a rifle slanted across his back, held by a sling.

Standing unseen inside the cabin, Jordan watched as his visitor threw a questioning glance in the direction of the corralled dun, then steered the calico with knee pressure toward the cabin door. Outside, he checked his mount with a jerk of rawhide reins and raised his voice, 'Hello, the house!'

'Howdy!' returned Jordan, stepping into the doorway.

The swarthy rider raised a hand in salutation and stepped off his pony. He was tall, loose-limbed and thin as a beanpole. And his eyes were a startling blue.

Half-breed, registered Jordan. 'Heard a shot,' said the stranger offhand. 'Figured I'd drift over for a look-see. The moniker's Irish.'

'I had an argument with a Turtle puncher,' explained Jordan. 'Bought Harker's place and craved the range cleared.'

'Bad medicine!' returned the tall breed. 'You buck the Turtle and you got trouble, big trouble.'

'I can handle it!' said Jordan shortly.

Irish focussed him in silence, no expression upon his long, bony features. 'Mebbe!' he said shortly.

'Rest your legs?' invited Jordan and

dropped onto the bench. Irish jackknifed beside him. They rolled smokes, each weighing the other.

Jordan learned that his visitor was a former U.S. Cavalry scout who had homesteaded the half-section beyond Cold Creek. Irish raised horses and sold them as remounts to government buyers.

Jordan told of his own plans to run stock. The tall breed asked no questions, but Jordan read guarded disbelief in his blue eyes. 'You claim I got trouble with the Turtle,' concluded Jordan. 'This Buck Burdock gent mean?'

'Meaner than a centipede with the chilblains,' Irish told him, 'and a range hog. There's three of us on this side of the river— me, old man Plummer west of me, and Razorback, up creek. We all got Turtle trouble. Guess Burdock ranges twenty thousand acres, but that ain't enough. He got to spill over onto our grass.'

'And you swallow it?' queried Jordan.

Irish raised bony shoulders. 'What kin we do? Burdock got ten *hombres* on his payroll. I fence a mite, but Burdock's as mean as a drunk squaw, always pushing, pushing. Plummer's ripe to quit.'

'I don't push easy,' commented Jordan.

'Burdock plays rough,' grunted Irish. He uncoiled his long form and stood, towering above Jordan. 'It sure is unhealthy around here!' With this cryptic utterance, he strode on

45

silent moccasins to his mount.

Jordan watched him drift away through the brush, sitting his mount bareback with effortless ease. This breed was a queer character. And just what did he mean by 'unhealthy'?

The cabin cleaning finished, the new owner of Harker's place arranged his stock of chuck on the shelves, filled the woodbox and cooked himself a meal. Then, as the sun dropped toward the bleak bulk of the San Marcos, he made a smoke, squatted on the bench that fronted the cabin and relaxed.

Before him stretched the grassy flat, specked with scrub oak, whose elongated shadows reached over the dried grass. Beyond, the surface of Sandy River lay like molten silver beneath the rays of the setting sun. Already, a scattering of steers had drifted back, eager to return to familiar graze. He'd have to fence the river front, decided Jordan, or he'd never be free of Turtle cows.

He liked this Arizona country, he decided. It was pleasant to get away from the scum that infested the border; pleasant to leave behind the fiery monotony of the desert; pleasant to listen to the purling of a creek and to eye green chaparral. His thoughts went to the hidden loot. Just where, he reflected idly, would an *hombre* with a posse biting his dust cache a quarter-million in gold and greenbacks? He'd scarcely have time to bury it.

Yet it must he in a safe spot, because Harker had been almighty sure it would not be found. A cave, maybe, close by, in the hills. He decided the terrain surrounding the cabin would stand a good combing over; not too close or too far. Harker had outfoxed the law, maybe he could outfox Harker.

Suddenly he tensed, at a quick flash high on a hillside, to the east. Could be a piece of broken glass, he ruminated, reflecting the sinking sun. Or it could be the lens of a spy-glass, carelessly exposed. Odds were someone was keeping cases on him. A shcriff's deputy, maybe, figuring Harker had sent him back to retrieve the loot. It might be a good idea if he fooled them for a while and went about stocking the ranch. Harker was dead, the loot was safc.

A purpling curtain shrouded the river and blotted out the hills as night thickened. He rose and stepped into the darkened cabin. There was oil in the stable lamp but he didn't bother to light it. Closing the door, he set a bar across it. Spread his soogans on the bunk, yanked off his boots and stretched out. Drifting off to sleep, he remembered Carol Hall's warning—to sleep in Harker's cabin meant sure death. In the darkness, he smiled. He'd show her!

A white, glowing shaft of sunlight, slanting through a small window, woke him. Outside, birds were twittering. Way off a bull rumbled challenge. Bluejays scolded around the eaves.

Yawning, he swung his legs down to the floor and reached for his boots. Well, it was sunup, he reflected, with amusement, and he was alive, very much alive. He'd sure proved the disciples of doom all wrong. As he'd figured, local folks had spread the yarn about sudden death to scare strangers away. The cabin was stuffy. He moved to the door, lifted down the bar and swung the door open. Filling his lungs with the rush of fresh air, he stepped across the threshold.

Bellied beside a manzanita on a slope not four hundred yards distant, the waiting marksman cuddled the stock of a Winchester to a shoulder, and squeezed the trigger.

Too late, Jordan, not yet wide awake, realized that he had forgotten the trench dug along the threshold. His right foot went down. Unbalanced, he plunged forward, sprawling on his face. And, as he fell, he heard the slap of a bullet slamming into the door jamb and the sharp crack of a Winchester resounded in his ears. Then he hit the ground with a bone-shaking thud. Suddenly very wide awake, he rolled fast. Another whining slug kicked dust, but he had rolled around the corner of the cabin and was hidden from his unknown assailant.

Dust-smothered, he lay lax, gasping for breath. Then he began to give thought to his predicament. This was one heck of a tight, he

48

considered stoically. Beyond the angle of the cabin a killer lay up on the hillside, Winchester levelled. He—Jordan—was unarmed. His gunbelt hung from a peg above the bunk and his rifle was propped in a corner by the stove. To reach either he had to enter by the doorway, which was as good as applying for a passport to hell. At any moment, too, the bushwhacking coyote might get a notion to drop down the hillside, round the cabin and blast him at pleasure. He was just about as helpless as a rabbit in a wolf's mouth. His one chance of survival was to find cover fast.

He scrambled to his feet and ducked around to the rear of the cabin. To his left, a verdant wall of chaparral marked the course of Cold Creek. But to reach its shelter he would be compelled to run a gauntlet of lead. Nothing offered across the flat to his right. That left the terrain in the rear of the cabin. This undulated in uneven waves, rising until it finally funnelled into a chaparral-choked ravine. Here was chance of cover and of escape.

At a run, he angled away from the cabin, scraping through thorny mesquite and dodging between the gnarled trunks of scrub oak. As he raced, his spine prickled. Very quickly, he knew, he would be beyond cover of the cabin and appear in the sights of the bushwhacker's Winchester. The prospect of a bullet in the back, or a smashed spine, was not pleasant. Zig-zagging, he dodged through the trees. For twenty or thirty paces there was silence, except for his labored breathing. Then a bullet abruptly plunked into a tree trunk beyond him and the crack of the detonation hit his ears.

Blindly, he swerved, frantically dodging and leaping over low brush. Another slug zipped through the twigs of a low-lying branch as he fended it aside in his headlong rush.

The brush thickened, and impeded his progress, but it also afforded a welcome screen. He dropped down and began to worm through it, angling off at a tangent to his former line of retreat and careful to make no disturbance that would telegraph his progress.

Two more shots, plainly thrown at random, followed. Then there was silence again as he snaked deeper and deeper into the brush. Finally, he stopped and lay flat on his belly beneath a lacery of branches. Quiet reigned, save for the twitter of birds.

Chest heaving, he waited, alert and tense as a hunted animal; but there were no signs of pursuit. Daylight strengthened. Distant peaks slowly turned to gold as the sun rimmed the hills.

Breathing easier now, the fugitive considered his next move. This had turned into a cat-and-mouse game. As long as he lay hidden, his assailant could perch up on the hillside, waiting. The first indication of movement would draw a stream of lead. He was pinned down and there was nothing he could do about it. His only chance lay in outwaiting the other. Bitterly, he regretted his carelessness in leaving the cabin without arms.

Time dragged, and the sun crept higher. Despite the partial protection of the brush, fiery rays bit through his shirt and seared his neck like a branding iron. A mottled whiptail lizard scurried past his nose and a sprightly rock wren perched on a nearby rock, summing him up with beady black eyes. Faintly, he could hear the murmur of Cold Creek and, as the heat built up, so did his thirst. He fought an urge to crawl toward the creek. That would be a fool play, reason told him. The *hombre* with the Winchester was waiting for just that very move.

Abruptly, he tensed as a yell reached his ears, 'Hey—Jordan! You around?' There was no mistaking the breed's deep voice. Was Irish the bushwhacker? Jordan's tongue was swelling and the heat blasted his back. Sound of shots had brought the breed yesterday, he reasoned. Maybe they had brought him again. He decided to gamble. Stiffly, he rose to his feet and began to push through the brush.

CHAPTER SIX

When he rounded the cabin, Irish was standing by the doorway, a rifle slanted beneath his right arm. At sight of the dishevelled Jordan, he stared, then his bronzed features crinkled with amusement. 'You look like the tail-end of a misspent night,' he commented.

'I feel like I had supper with a coyote,' croaked Jordan. He ducked into the cabin, buckled on his gunbelt and dipped a tin mug into the water bucket. Feeling better, he stepped outside again.

'What brought you around?' he asked.

'Shots!' replied Irish shortly. 'You started another war?'

'Nope, a stranger figured on sending me to hell on a shutter.' He told of the bushwhacker. 'The way it looks, some skunk from the Turtle craved to salivate me,' he wound up.

'There's others around,' said Irish.

'Who else would crave my scalp?'

'Harker's pards, Joe Leggett and Bill Negg.'

'Ain't the Law on their trail?'

'Sure!' grunted the breed. 'But the Law's in Clearwater, a day's ride distant, and the boys been ducking around the Bad Lands.' He jerked his head in the direction of the angle of upended terrain that lay to the north. 'Wal, just where was this gent holed up?'

'From the gun flash, halfway up the hill.' Jordan nodded at the slope to the west, the creek curling around its base.

Without further talk, Irish led the way to the creek, Jordan hastening behind to keep up with the long, silent strides. They forded the creek and began to climb the slope.

'Rest awhile,' directed Irish. 'Could be you'll muss the sign.' He pulled ahead, criss-crossing the slope, searching. Finally he paused, and beckoned. Jordan scrambled up.

Close by the breed, jagged rock projected from the red soil and, beneath a lacy mesquite, several shell cases glinted in the sunlight. Jordan started forward to pick them up but Irish thrust out a long arms and restrained him. He handed the rider his gun, and Jordan noted that it was a Spencer single-shot, an old cavalry carbine. Those shell cases had been ejected from a Winchester .44.

Irish dropped onto hands and knees and began carefully examining the sandy ground, crawling around, peering and poking. Finally, he uncoiled his elongated form, came to his feet and dusted off his levis. 'I'd say the *hombre* stood 5' 6", mebb'e 5' 8",' he commented. 'Not heavy built. Wore riding boots. Hung around quite a while, half-smoked five quirlies; could be he was a mite edgy. He left in a hell of a hurry.'

'What's the color of his hair?' inquired Jordan gravely.

'Sandy, and his eyes are gray,' returned Irish imperturbably. 'Lead-gray, like a slug. He got a thin, pock-marked face and two buck teeth. That is, if my guess hits the bull's-eye. I'm thinking it was Joe Leggett.'

'One of Harker's pards?'

The breed nodded.

'And the skunk's deep in the malpais by now?'

'Mebbeso,' agreed the other, 'but I reckon he'll be back.'

'So that's why you figure Harker's place unhealthy?' said Jordan thoughtfully. 'You coulda said more.'

'It ain't my fight,' responded the breed gruffly. 'Wal, I got bronks to break!' He turned away.

'I'll side you aways,' offered Jordan. 'Got a yen to brace this Plummer gent and take them steers off his hands'

'Wal, you're sure no quitter,' acknowledged the breed and led the way downhill.

Cy Plummer proved to be a gaunt, rheumy-eyed homesteader, aging, with a sorrowful mien and a shock of greasy, uncombed beard. His half-section lay a mile up river, beyond Irish's layout. It was mostly open pasture and it was crowded with Turtle cows.

At the sound of Jordan's approach, he emerged from a brush hoogan, a frowsy, unkempt figure, stinking of rotgut. Nearby, a hobbled, spur-scratched old cow pony nuzzled

54

grass.

The homesteader's bleary eyes brightened at the prospect of selling his stock. Yes, he owned fifteen or twenty head of yearlings, maybe more, he admitted vaguely. He hadn't made a tally in a coon's age. Prime stock, wouldn't part with a single critter, but he had a yen to drift. The price was $25 apiece.

Jordan shrugged and offered $15 apiece—take it or leave it—and the oldtimer eagerly snapped up the offer. His stock was mixed up with Turtle stuff, he said. It would take quite a while to cut them out.

'Deliver 'em at Harker's place within two days,' directed Jordan briskly, 'or no deal.' Curiously, he inquired, 'You lease your graze to the Turtle?'

'The Turtle lease graze!' cackled Plummer. 'That's sure a lapaloozer, mister. The Turtle don't lease—it grabs.'

'You could fence!'

'Tried it oncet, but Burdock don't abide fences. Promised to fit me with a rawhide necktie if I didn't drop the crazy notion.'

'Irish fences!'

'Wal,' admitted Plummer. 'The Turtle's kinda partial to the breed. Burdock uses him occasional to bust bronks.'

'So that's why he sticks around!'

'I got a notion,' confided the oldster, 'that Irish figures to nose out the loot Harker cached. Thet Apache's sly, and he kin track a

55

wood tick over solid rock.'

Riding back along the river bank to his newly acquired spread, Jordan pondered on the old homesteader's remarks concerning Irish. Seemed the breed was another he'd have to watch out for. That made three men with designs on the loot, not counting Sheriff Haslipp and his deputies. And the Turtle was liable to kick back any time. Burdock and his crew apparently made their own law along the river and they sure wouldn't stomach the winging of Sudden. Before he located that quarter-million, he thought whimsically, he'd probably earn it.

With nightfall he draped the two windows and lit the stable lamp. His silhouette made too tempting a target in the yellow glow of the lamp. The stars flamed thick across the velvet-blue of the night sky when he blew out the lamp, eased open the cabin door and slid outside. A blanket was rolled, bandolier fashion, over one shoulder, and he packed his Winchester. Ghosting through the shadows, he hit for the hillside upon which the would-be assassin had sprawled. If the bushwhacker tried his luck again, he craved to be in a position where he could retaliate.

Questing over the slope, he picked a spot amid a tumbled pile of rock, above and beyond the bushwhacker's eyrie. First beating the ground with the rolled blanket to scare off any lurking rattlesnakes, he settled down and, in minutes, was asleep.

Stars were fading and the grayness of dawn clung like a mist to the hillside when Jordan blinked awake, limbs stiff with cold. Peering down slope, he could distinguish nothing but dark blotches that were patches of brush. Hunkered against a boulder, he made a cigarette, remembered, and chewed it cold, setting himself to wait until the light strengthened.

Oncoming day slowly erased the shadows. The river gleamed below, steers standing hock-deep along its margin. Eastward, the jagged outline of the Black Kaweahs was black-etched against the rising sun.

Scanning the bleak hillside, still flecked with shadow, Jordan could see nothing that moved. Then, distinct through the stillness, a metallic click reached his ears. Someone close by had levered a cartridge into the breach of a rifle. Taut now, he froze, eyes straining. Abruptly, he focused the outline of a man, clad in range garb, lying motionless beside an outcrop of eroding rock, not thirty paces below him—the exact spot where he and Irish had found the shell cases the previous morning.

Bellied flat, a Winchester held loosely to his shoulder, the stranger was watching the cabin. His back made a tempting target. Silently, Jordan aligned his rifle. The prone form lay square in the sights. Then, with a sigh, he lowered the barrel. He just couldn't bring

57

himself to plug an unsuspecting stranger in the back, even though that stranger plainly planned to kill him. Quietly, on all fours, he squirmed between boulders and began to Injun downhill.

Foot by foot, he slithered down toward the would-be bushwhacker. He was almost within reach of the stranger's scuffed riding boots when, for no apparent reason, the man's head jerked around and Jordan stared into a pair of startled lead-gray eyes, deepset in pocked features. A bristly fringe of beard decorated the lantern jaw and a thin-lipped mouth gaped with surprise, revealing two prominent buck teeth.

'You make one move,' promised Jordan starkly, 'and I'll sure drill you, plumb between the buttocks.' He came to his feet and, covering the prone man, advanced and kicked the Winchester out of reach.

'On your feet!' he barked.

Gnawing his underlip, the other rose, slowly and stiffly.

'Unbuckle that gunbelt!' Jordan's Winchester slanted on the pock-faced man's chest.

Reluctantly, the other loosened his gunbelt and it dropped.

'Now step back—way back!' growled Jordan, advancing and prodding the fellow's belly with the muzzle of his Winchester.

Still not speaking, the man shuffled

backward.

Jordan scooped up the gunbelt and slung it over a shoulder. 'So you're Joe Leggett!' he commented, with disgust. 'Just a yellow, lousy bushwhacker. You know any prayers—spit 'em out.'

'Quit dribbling and plug me!' rasped the pock-faced man.

'Could be your carcass would be good for nothing but buzzard bait,' mused Jordan. 'I don't recollect if that reward dodger read "$1,000-dead or alive".'

The other stood gnawing at his underlip. Blood began to trickle down his unshaven chin.

'Maybe I should take you in,' decided Jordan. 'I sure would hate to forfeit that thousand. Where's your saddle-horse?'

The pock-faced man stood scowling, thin lips locked. Jordan shrugged. 'Wal, leg it—downhill.'

He saw the would-be killer relax with a quick release of breath. Leggett pivoted and began to plod toward the creek, sparkling below.

Outside the cabin, Jordan trussed his prisoner's arms behind him with a rawhide strap that Leggett used as belt. 'You move and your pants will slide down and hobble you,' he observed, and headed for the corral.

In no haste, he saddled the dun, rode out, fashioned a noose with his rope, dropped it

59

over the prisoner's head and jerked the loop tight. 'You got two options.' he drawled. 'Leg it to Clearwater, or lead me to your bronk. I ain't particular which.'

With a snarl, Leggett led the way back toward the creek. His pony, a fleabitten bronk, was tied in a draw behind a shoulder of the hill.

It was near sundown when those citizens of Clearwater who were dawdling beneath the store canopies stared at a strange sight. Two trail-stained riders stirred the dust of Main Street. First rode a pock-faced man, wrists lashed to the saddlehorn and a noose tight around his scrawny throat. Tailing him, the rope dallied around his horn, rode a gray-shirted rider wearing corduroy pants.

Eyes followed the pair as they wheeled to the rail outside the courthouse. Word spread around town, as fast as a brush fire, 'Some gent brought in Joe Leggett!'

Sheriff Haslipp bulked at his desk and the leathery-faced deputy known as Pecos sprawled on a straightback chair when Jordan ushered his prisoner into the office.

'Holy rattlesnake's puppies!' ejaculated Pecos.

At the exclamation, the sheriff swung around, took in the roped prisoner and his escort. 'Wal, if it ain't Joe Leggett!' he commented. 'Nice work, Jordan!'

The rider shook his loop loose and carefully

60

coiled the rope. 'If you can't tie him in with the hold-up,' he said casually, 'I'll file a complaint—attempted murder.' He told of the shots.

'We got plenty on Joe,' returned Haslipp grimly. 'If he dodges the rope, he'll rot in Yuma. Search him and book the skunk, Pecos!'

Jordan watched as the deputy expertly relieved the sullen prisoner of jackknife, a block of stinkers, the makin's and some loose change. Then he hustled Leggett out of the office.

Jordan still lingered, eying the gallery of 'wanted' notices tacked on the wall.

'You don't have to stick around and sign a complaint,' said the sheriff. 'Like I said, we already got enough on Joe to hang him.'

'That ain't bothering me,' admitted Jordan.

'But the bounty is!' Haslipp chuckled. 'Don't fret! You'll draw that thousand—on conviction.'

Jordan nodded, and turned to leave. Haslipp's voice checked him, 'You got any heirs?'

'Just why would I need heirs?' demanded the rider.

'To claim that bounty,' returned the lawman dryly. 'Bill Negg is still loose. Bill and Joe are as close as the twin barrels of a scattergun. And Bill's a killer! Then I hear you been prodding the Turtle. When you tangle with Buck Burdock you got a grizzly on your hands.

61

You're pushing your luck, Jordan!'

'Wal, what would you figure I should do about it?' queried the rider, poker-faced.

'Beat it back to the Rio Grande—pronto,' advised Haslipp. 'Don't bank on Lady Luck aceing you out of any more tights.'

'I'll chew on the notion awhile,' smiled Jordan.

The sheriff raised his broad shoulders. 'Ain't no chewing —in boothill.'

Outside the courthouse, Jordan paused and his glance flicked up and down the dusty street. Though he would never have admitted it, he was hoping to sight a trim figure in white shirtwaist and dark skirt. But there was no sign of the attractive school ma'am.

Reluctant to leave, he stabled his pony at the livery, saw that it was watered and fed, then wandered down to the Maverick Saloon.

The drink emporium was no different from a score of others in which he had wet his throat. There was the customary ornate backbar mirror, lithochromes of luscious nudes on the walls, brass oil lamps hanging from the rafters, and the customary stale stench—a composite of cigarette smoke, spilt whisky and unwashed bodies—hung on the air.

He bought a mug of beer at the bar and retired to a side table. From habit, he idly watched the yammering groups hunched around small tables scattered over the sanded floor, and the row of shirt-sleeved townsmen bellied up to the bar.

A jolly, roly-poly individual, with a round moon face, caught his attention. The fat man was circulating around, exchanging chit-chat with the patrons. He affected a gambler's sober black broadcloth and starched white shirt. The diamond in his stickpin, considered Jordan, was as large as a locomotive headlight.

Unexpectedly, the object of the rider's attention plumped down on a chair opposite and eyed Jordan's half empty beer mug. His gaze rose to focus the rider and Jordan saw that his eyes, small and bedded in fat, were as hard as chips of agate, belying the amiable smile that crinkled his fleshy features.

'So you brought in Joe Leggett!' he piped, in shrill, penetrating tones. 'That calls for a drink—on the house.' He raised his voice, 'Scotty! A bottle of bourbon, the best, and a glass.'

A dour-faced bartender set the bottle and glass on the table. The fat man poured, liberally, and pushed the glass toward Jordan. 'They call me Keeno,' he volunteered affably. 'I own the joint.'

Jordan nodded and sipped. When he set the glass down, the fat man was ready with an open cigar case, his triple chins quivering with joviality. Just what was behind this unwonted hospitality, wondered Jordan, and accepted a cigar. The question was soon answered.

'They claim you settled on Jed Harker's

place,' said Keeno.

'Just figure on running a few steers,' returned Jordan, offhand.

'I'd say you handle a gun better'n a branding iron,' beamed the fat man.

'What give you that idea?'

The saloon man glanced at the tied-down gun, and smiled. 'Wal,' he replied, 'things get around. That Turtle fracas, for instance. And what homesteader could bring in Joe Leggett?' He sobered and his voice dropped. 'Let's spread the cards! My guess is that a quarter-million loot brought you to Jed's place. It'll be tough to get away, with that foxy sheriff keeping cases on every move you make. You need a sidekick, to lend a hand when the time's ripe.'

'So?' questioned Jordan.

The saloon man beamed. 'Keeno never let a pard down. Slip it to me, in small instalments. I'll handle the getaway chore.'

'Your cut?'

The fat man spread his white hands deprecatingly. 'Is Keene a hog? Twenty-five percent!'

'That sounds real interesting,' murmured the rider. 'Right now, maybe you could help, with a little advice.'

'Sure!' returned Keeno expansively.

'That breed, whose place sits next to Harker's. I just don't figure the gent.'

'Irish!' Keeno smiled. 'No one figures Irish.

Some claim he had a hand in the hold-up, but not when he's around.'

'Any evidence?'

'Nothing! 'Cept Harker was his neighbor, and they're cousins.'

With that the saloon man rose and waved airily at the bottle of bourbon. 'It's all yours,' he beamed. 'on the house.' Features creased with amiability, he waddled away.

So maybe Irish was tied in with the hold-up gang, pondered Jordan. That didn't sound good, and it didn't square with his actions the morning of the attempted bushwhacking. Then it could be Irish was hunting the loot himself and figured that he—Jordan—was acquainted with its location. Odds were that the breed had combed Harker's place pretty thoroughly—with no luck. So now he was banking on this *hombre* from the Rio Grande to lead him to it. Which mcant that Irish wanted him kept alive.

One thing was sure. There were a slug of *hombres* interested in that quarter-million.

CHAPTER SEVEN

Daylight was fading when Jordan returned to Harker's place, the following day. Cows again dotted the flat. It was plain that Turtle stock was returning to familiar graze. Those cows would prove a pest, considered the rider. He'd never be rid of Burdock's beef unless he fenced the river front. He blinked as the dun jogged closer to the cabin. A buggy with fringed top was drawn up to the door and a townsman, placidly smoking a pipe, sat on the bench.

Wondering who in creation his visitor might be, Jordan dismounted at the corral, shucked saddle and bridle and spread the sweated saddle blanket over the top rail. When he approached the cabin, his visitor rose languidly. 'Wonderful evening!' he exclaimed. 'Marvellous view! Fascinating country!'

Jordan's glance travelled over him, trying to figure his business. He had all the earmarks of a city man, and a decided British accent. Of medium height, he was stockily built and inclined to plumpness. A neat mustache, well waxed, ornamented his ruddy features. The tweed suit he wore was carefully tailored, his white silk shirt spotless and his striped tie conservative. A stylish cream Stetson lay on the bench.

Somehow, Jordan was reminded of a plump partridge.

At the puzzled inquiry in the rider's eyes, his visitor smiled apologetically, soft brown eyes guileless. 'Merely a business call,' he volunteered. 'You might term me an itinerant photographer, questing for business.' He proffered an oblong piece of pasteboard, with a courteous bow. Jordan took it and read:

REGINALD CHUMBLEY
Photographer
Groups a Specialty

'Wal, Reggie,' he drawled, 'I'd say you're as likely to locate business around here as to find oysters in the desert. You belong in town. There's no dinero to be made out here.'

'Money, my friend,' returned the other, with a tolerant smile, 'is merely a means to an end. The end is existence, and it requires precious little money to exist. My camera merely supplies the necessities. My satisfactions come from solitude, the primitive, the even tenor of a pastoral life.'

Jordan assimilated these remarks and they didn't make good sense. 'Ain't you scairt to mosey around wild country naked?' he queried.

The other frowned with puzzlement, glanced down at his well-brushed tweeds. 'Naked, old chap?

67

'Without a gun!'

'Oh, a picturesque allusion!' He smiled disarmingly. 'I detest lethal weapons.' Somewhat abruptly, he changed the subject, 'You'd probably treasure a picture of your cabin, your pony, possibly your good self?'

'Nope!' decided Jordan. 'But you earned a supper and a shakedown for driving out here. Loose your pony in the corral and stay the night.'

'Sorry, old chap,' returned the other regretfully. 'I plan to spend the night with Mr. Irish. Remarkable fellow, Irish.' He followed Jordan into the cabin and stood chatting while the rider started a fire in the stove. It appeared that he had already driven up river and made the acquaintance of Irish and Cy Plummer. 'The environment appeals,' enthused Chumbley. 'Never have I discovered such rustic charm, such vistas, such tranquility.'

Frying up bacon and beans, Jordan considered wryly that the tranquility had somehow eluded him.

After eating, the Englishman scraped back his chair, apologizing profusely for his haste. 'I promised friend Irish I would be back before nightfall,' he concluded, 'but we shall probably see more of each other.'

'You sticking around?' inquired Jordan, with a quick, questioning glance.

'Possibly,' beamed Chumbley.

Thoughtfully, the rider gazed after his

voluble visitor as the buggy bounced away. Granted that all Limeys were crazy, this Chumbley gent just didn't make sense. He was just too artless, too confiding. And he sure wouldn't do enough business on the river to buy beans.

Jordan set to work with a shovel, filling the checkerboard of holes around the cabin, and forgot his visitor.

At sunup, the scolding of jays around the eaves awoke him and he lay, half asleep, muscles sore from the spade work.

The muted thud of ponies' hooves brought him to a sitting position. He tumbled off the bunk, stepped to a window and peered out. Remnants of night still clung to the hollows, but a bunch of riders jingling up from the river were plain. He swiftly tallied them—five, six, seven. 'The Turtle!' he muttered, watching them fan out in a half-circle in front of the cabin, check their mounts and sit stolidly waiting. A bull voice resounded, 'Jordan—come on out!'

He yanked on his boots. buckled on his gunbelt, dropped the bar and swung the door open. Hands on hips, he stood surveying the semi-circle of poker-faced punchers. Slightly ahead, forking a black stallion, was a heavy-set rider, bull-necked and heavy jowled. His weathered features were as dark as old cowhide and stamped with intolerance, but there was not a weak spot on them. He was clad in puncher garb, differing from the others only in that he wore a sleeveless leather vest. A gun was buckled around his thick middle.

He fixed Jordan with a frowning stare.

'Wal,' drawled the rider, 'I'm out—so what?' This, he guessed, would be Buck Burdock, boss of the Turtle.

'Vamoose!' roared the rancher. He fished out a fat silver-cased watch. 'You got five minutes to haul your duds out of that shack and hightail afore I set a torch to it.'

'You're trespassing!'

'Quit dribbling and rattle your hocks,' growled the big man.

'If you say so,' returned Jordan resignedly and turned to re-enter the cabin. Then, in a flash, he whirled, gun in hand. And it was lined on the rancher. His action had been so swift and so unexpected that not a rider stirred.

'Now you listen, Burdock,' he said brittlely. 'Just one move, you or your boys and a slug blasts through your guts. Sheriff Haslipp got a deputy on that hill.' he jerked his head eastward, 'keeping cases on me. He'll back my claim it was self-defense. Now I give you two minutes—get off this spread or swallow a pill you won't digest.'

Time ticked away as he met Burdock's unwinking stare. There was no sound except the creak of saddle leather as punchers shifted uneasily in their saddles. Finally, Jordan added casually, 'I reckon your time's most run out.'

'My boys will make a sieve out of you,' rasped Burdock.

'Will that help you any?' mocked Jordan.

For perhaps ten seconds the rancher considered this, his eyes on the levelled .45. Then, abruptly, he wheeled away. His punchers dropped in behind him and, a jingling cavalcade, they cantered across the flat toward the river.

Jordan stood watching them. He'd bluffed Burdock this time, he reflected, but this wasn't the last of the affair. The heavy-jawed rancher wasn't the type to acccpt a repulse. The Turtle would be back.

He spun around as another pony racked out of the brush by the creek and cycloned toward him. Sitting in the saddle was a slim rider, wearing denims and a checked flannel shirt. Then he grasped that it was a girl with oval features, her brown hair unconfined and streaming in the breeze. Scattering dust and pebbles, she yanked the pony to a sliding stop in front of the astonished Jordan and swung lightly out of the saddle. His eyes widened. It was the school ma'am, Carol Hall.

'You were wonderful!' she ejaculated breathlessly. 'You made that Burdock brute eat crow.' Her eyes were shining. 'That big bully,' she continued, 'has tormented the small ranchers along the river for ycars and no one ever had the sand to stand up to him. How did you do it?'

'Got the drop on him!' he threw back tersely.

'You defied seven riders!' she enthused. 'I could scarcely believe my eves.'

'What in creation are you doing up here?' he demanded, anxious to change the subject.

'Why, I live here,' she laughed.

'Seems to me you claimed to be the school ma'am, in town,' he accused.

'I am! And I have a room in Mrs. Holiday's boarding house. Weekends I spend with my brother. He raises hogs, up creek.'

'Razorback?'

She nodded.

He stood rasping his chin and wishing he'd had time to shave. 'Well,' she demanded, 'do we eat? I rode over for breakfast.'

'Sure, sure!' he returned hastily, scarce crediting his good fortune. He moved aside and indicated the open doorway. 'Step in, ma'am!'

'Let's make it Carol,' she returned, and added roguishly, 'Do I still call you *Mister* Jordan?'

'Bill!' he threw back, grabbed the empty water bucket and made a beeline for the creek.

When he returned, Carol was busy at the stove. He led her roan over to the corral, slacked its cinches, watered it and tied it in the shade. Hurrying back at her hail, he found flapjacks browning on the stove, bacon sputtering and the coffee pot bubbling.

Never had he enjoyed breakfast more. The dishes washed, they sat on the bench outside.

'Any luck?' she inquired unexpectedly.

'Luck?' Jordan eyed her innocently.

'As if you didn't know what I mean,' she smiled.

'Cy Plummer sold me twenty head, yearlings, if he can locate 'em.'

'So that's your cover!'

'You got me buffaloed, Ma—Miss Carol,' he confessed.

She eyed him with amusement. 'Still running a bluff! Well, Bill, promise me if you should, er, stumble, across Harker's loot you'll turn it over to the sheriff.'

'What else could a good citizen do?' he inquired blandly.

She sighed. 'That's the trouble. I'm not altogether convinced that you are a good citizen.' She came to her feet and extended a slim hand. 'Well, I must be riding. Drop over to our place some weekend. Just follow the creek.'

'I sure will!' he assured her fervently.

Around noon, Cy Plummer drifted into view, hazing a small bunch of steers. He threw them onto the flat and headed for the cabin, outside of which Jordan was still filling holes.

The homesteader stepped out of his applejack saddle and ground-hitched the ancient cow pony. 'Couldn't locate more'n ten of the critters,' he confessed mournfully. 'Irish

73

vent-branded 'em. I got no iron.'

Jordan counted $150 in greenbacks into the oldster's grimy palm and pocketed a scribbled bill of sale. 'You drifting?' he asked casually.

'Reckon I'll rest up in town awhile,' returned the graying homesteader. 'Done leased my half-section to some loco Limey. Sure glad to be shut of it.'

'Leased to who?' inquired Jordan sharply.

'Mister Reginald Chumbley,' said Plummer, a spark of humor in his rheumy eyes. 'Packs a big camera around. Right now he's dickering with Irish to build him a shack.' He hauled himself into the saddle and drifted away.

So the Limey was locating on Plummer's place, mused Jordan. Why? It seemed almighty curious that the so-called photographer had wandered in at this time. It was also more curious that, despite his asserted loathing for lethal weapons, he packed a hideaway beneath his tweed coat, under his left arm.

CHAPTER EIGHT

Night enfolded Clearwater and its citizens slept, with the exception of the more thirsty, who occasionally banged through the batwings of the Maverick.

The courthouse stood darkened and silent as a tomb, except for a glow that illuminated one narrow side window. This glow marked the location of the sheriff's office, where two men were engaged in serious confab. One was Haslipp himself and the other a smooth-featured, urbane individual with sharp eyes and a jovial smile. At a casual glance most men would have placed Sam Leppman as a cattle buyer or a drummer; he had the easy, affable manner of a salesman. Slipped beneath the sweatband of his natty gray Stetson, however, was a small metal badge, quickly available for identification. It bore the stamped inscription: Pinkerton. #875.

Haslipp drew contemplatively upon a cigar. 'So your boys finally caught up with Harker?'

Leppman smiled gently. 'In a manner of speaking, yes. But Harker was in no shape to sing. Someone had planted a knife between his shoulder blades. A mestizo found the body floating down the Rio Grande, below a small pueblo called Santa Monte.'

The sheriff nodded, 'It makes sense.'

'Its harder to pry information out of Santa Monte than find hair on a frog,' continued Leppman, 'but we did discover that Harker had been hanging around the cantina, drinking hard. Seems there was some kind of a fracas. He and this Jordan *hombre* slipped out the back.' He paused. 'There the trail ended, 'til Harker's body turned up.'

'Plain as the ears on a mule,' contributed Haslipp. 'Harker yawped too much and spilled the beans. This Jordan is as coldblooded as a rattlesnake. He persuaded Harker to sign over the half-section, stuck the coyote and dumped the carcass in the river.'

'Dog eat dog!' said Leppman benignly.

'You got anything else on Jordan?' inquired the sheriff.

'Not a thing,' admitted the Pinkerton man. 'Talk was he ran wet stock. It's a safe bet he was on the lam. Who else would stick around Santa Monte?'

'I wonder just how much the lobo knows?' murmured Haslipp.

'Plenty, I'd say. If he scared Harker into signing a deed, odds are he dug the location of the cache out of him. Give one of them border wolves a knife and he'll make a graven image talk.'

'So the gent could lift that loot any time?'

'Any time!' smiled Leppman. 'Just waiting for a chance to slip away.'

'Wal, he won't get far,' commented the

sheriff complacently. 'The San Marcos block him to the west. North, he'd curl up in the Barrens, no water, no trails. East, we got the passes over the Kaweahs covered. That leaves the south, desert country, the trail Harker took. I got men posted at the waterholes .' He eyed the Pinkerton man with heavy satisfaction. 'I figure we got the *hombre* hogtied.'

'Could be!' agreed Leppman amicably. 'But 'til that lobo makes a move, you're hogtied.'

'Sure as shooting,' grunted Haslipp. 'We want the loot. Bring in Jordan and he'd dumb up, tighter than a drum.'

'So,' smiled Leppman, 'we have to persuade the gent to light out. Right? Well, I think I can handle that chore.' He answered the question in Haslipp's eyes. 'We'll throw a scare into the *hombre.*'

'He don't scare easy.'

The Pinkerton mail chuckled, 'Every man values his own skin. Guess I'll ride up river. Could be I could peddle a little barbed wire.'

'Barbed wire?'

'That's my cover—salesman—Whirlaway Windmills and Wait-a-Bit Barbed Wire. It's good most anywhere.'

*　　*　　*

Jordan was engaged in the unending chore of pushing Turtle cows back across the river

77

when Sam Leppman jogged along the trail. Cows, like most animals, are creatures of habit. Loose a pony miles away from its corral and it will drift hack; haze a cow far away from familiar graze and it will ultimately return. Turtle stock was no exception to the rule, and the new owner of Harker's place was almighty tired of running Burdock's beef off his grass.

Leppman rode up as Jordan paused on the river bank, resting his blowing pony after chasing a particularly stubborn steer.

'Howdy!' greeted the visitor cheerily. He eyed the sweating pony and the cows bawling across stream. 'Neighbor's cows pesky?'

'Pesky!' growled Jordan. 'A swarm of hornets couldn't be worse.'

'Then apparently I arrived at an opportune moment,' beamed Leppman. 'My line is barbed wire, Wait-a-Bit barbed wire, best brand on the market. Wait-a-Bit wire will hold a herd of elephants. Galvanized for lifetime service, double-barbed, heat-treated.' He cast an appraising glance along the river front. 'Six spools, maybe seven, and your problem is solved; your worries are over.'

'I've been chewing on the idea,' confessed Jordan. 'Let's mosey over to the cabin.'

The deal concluded and arrangements made for wire and posts to be freighted out, the affable Leppman remained for supper. Jordan found him good company. After eating, they rolled smokes and relaxed. 'You know,' commented Leppman thoughtfully, 'a customer is a customer. He helps me, I like to help him. His back trail is none of my business, if you get me.'

Jordan detected something behind the words. 'Suppose you cut the deck a mite deeper,' he suggested.

Leppman shrugged. 'I poke around, pick up an order here, an order there. On occasion I pick up something I wasn't looking for.'

'Such as?'

The other smiled, 'Windies, mostly. F'r instance, I split a bottle with that sheriff in Clearwater. It kinda loosened his tongue. He let drop he'd just got word they'd trailed Harker, who held up a train hereabouts, to the border. Seems he was fished out of the Rio Grande, a knife in his back.' Leppman glanced at Jordan, who was listening politely. 'The sheriff had the idea,' he continued, 'that the gent who knifed Harker had good reason to be acquainted with the location of the bank loot. Didn't you ride up from the river?'

Jordan smiled and nodded.

'Quite a coincidence!' murmured Leppman. 'Wal, the sheriff plans on picking up the killer—pronto.' He came to his feet. 'Guess I'll drift and drop in on some of your neighbors. Could be they might use a little wire.'

When the hoofbeats of Leppman's pony died, Jordan sat considering the oblique warning. Seemed Sheriff Haslipp had him pegged for Harker's killing, which was natural, under the circumstances. But, lacking witnesses, the lawman would never make the charge stick. Haslipp had enough circumstantial evidence, however, to clap a man in the hoosegow and hold him for trial. That would end all chance of locating the loot.

But the longer he considered the possibility of arrest, the more Jordan became convinced that the sheriff would take no action. He figured Haslipp was a shrewd old law hound. It would bring him no praise if he arrested the alleged murderer of a wanted and hated man. The big feather in his cap would be recovery of the loot. And his only chance of recovering the loot was to wait until Jordan revealed its location. The sheriff would play it cagey—wait and watch. He'd postpone that arrest until he could grab both the gold and the suspected killer in one swoop.

But it was plain, decided Jordan, that he'd have to get busy and poke around. Haslipp's patience might run out.

The following morning he began to look the terrain over carefully. Harker, he reasoned, had a posse on his tail and little time to cache his loot. Therefore, it could not be far from the cabin. The cabin and barn had been most pulled to pieces by former searchers and the ground around them thoroughly dug over. That left the creek, winding between high cutbanks; the grass flat reaching to the river, and the rough, brushy terrain east and north of the cabin, slanting up into boulder-pitted hills and compressing in the rear to an arid canyon. It would consume weeks, months, to cover all likely ground thoroughly. He'd just have to guess and trust that a hunch would prove out.

As a starter, why not investigate the scrub oaks that dotted the flat? Any man hiding treasure would need a marker, and what better marker than a selected oak?

Pick in hand, Jordan began to work across the flat, from oak to oak, hunting for loose or misplaced earth, some kind of a monument, any kind of a clue. He was still searching when a wagon rolled along the river trail behind two straining horses, spools of barbed wire and posts bumping in the bed. Turtle cows were again thick upon the flat. He postponed his search and set to work digging post holes.

Stripped to the waist, he was stringing black and prickly wire when another visitor bulged into view. This neck of the woods, he considered irately, was becoming as crowded as Main Street. When the stranger checked nearby, he eyed the newcomer with puzzled amazement. Never had he seen the like.

Straddling a shaggy mule was a big, gaunt, rawboned fellow with a bushy beard and a mane of jet-black hair that curled to his shoulders. He used no saddle and his long legs almost brushed the ground on each side of the mule's barrel. Wide open, a cheap cotton shirt

81

exposed a thatch of dark hair on a barrel chest. Shabby pants were secured by a strip of rawhide and their bottoms thrust into dilapidated high boots. He wore an ill-fitting rusty-black frock coat, the two tails of which flopped down on either side of his mount, like broken wings. The coat was unbuttoned, revealing a heavy gunbelt buckled around his waist. One hand, with long bony fingers, grasped the reins, while the other arm was crooked, nursing a ponderous book.

The stranger returned Jordan's puzzled glance with two piercing dark eyes, twin pieces of jet set in the dark mahogany of his features. Below them arched a curved beak of a nose, which brought the thought of a questing hawk into Jordan's mind.

'For what hath man for all his labor and vexation if he fails to find salvation?' Deep and forceful, the bearded man's voice boomed from his mighty chest.

'All I got is blisters,' growled Jordan. 'And just who might you be, mister?'

'I am Paul the Preacher, brother, a humble servant of the Lord, carrying the glorious message of salvation to erring souls.' With this pronouncement, the rawboned man slid off the mule. In the depths of Jordan's mind, recollection stirred: a vague notion that he had met this man somewhere before. But, try as he would, the memory refused to be brought into focus.

'Ain't we met before?' he inquired, his brow creased.

'Brother,' boomed Paul, 'the sower spreadeth the Word in sundry places. I have cast the good seed from the Rio Grande to the Red River, from Santa Fe to the Sierras. Alas, most fell upon stony ground. Have you seen the Light, or do the flames of deepest Hell await you?'

Jordan smeared mingled sweat and grime from his forehead with a wry grin. 'Guess I got too much on my mind right now to bother about the Hereafter.'

'Wretched unbeliever, would you fry in Hell?' roared Paul.

'I'm too doggone busy to give it thought,' snapped Jordan. He bent and grasped a spool. 'Right now I got wire to string.'

Unexpectedly, the Preacher's voice dropped to the casual, 'And could well use another pair of hands,' he commented. 'Help one another! So saith the Lord.'

Without further ado, he set his ponderous book on a rock, slipped off his dangling frock coat and rolled up his shirt sleeves, exposing two muscular forearms. Then he went to work.

CHAPTER NINE

Before the rawboned preacher had labored long, Jordan was compelled to admit to himself that Paul was worth any two men. Strong as a freight ox and oblivious to the fiery sun, he worked unceasingly. Together, they dug post holes, set posts, unwound wire from the cumbersome wooden spools, strung and tacked it. Before sundown, the job was finished. Jordan, muscles aching from the effort to keep up with his helper, breathed a fervent sigh of relief. Paul shrugged into his rusty frock coat, seemingly as fresh as when he rode up. Together, they headed for the cabin, the mule plodding at the Preacher's heels like a huge shaggy dog.

The tantalizing memory that had eluded Jordan crystallized as they washed up at the bench. 'Dammit, I got you pegged now!' he exclaimed, swinging around to face the bearded man.

'Let he who would accuse first give thought to his own misdeeds,' boomed Paul, something akin to amusement in his piercing eyes.

'Sam Larson, alias Scripture Sam!' said Jordan. 'I lamped you in Santa Monte, dodging warrants for robbery with violence, bank holdups. That beard threw me off.'

'We do err and stray like lost sheep,'

intoned Paul, unabashed. 'It is true, brother. I confess to my shame that I once consorted with evil men, and my ways were an abomination in the sight of the Lord. Now,' he flexed his brawny arms, 'I have seen the Light. Repent, saith the Lord, and thy sins shall be forgiven. Once I was as black as Lucifer, now I am as white as snow.' Dropping his tone to the conversational, he added offhand, 'Would you hold a man's past against him?'

'I guess not,' admitted Jordan. But he wondered if the conversion was as complete as the bearded man claimed. Could the presence of a quarter-million loot account for his sudden appearance in Copper Valley?

But the loot was apparently far from the Preacher's thoughts. He inquired as to nearby neighbors and announced his intention of spreading the Good Word among them. That night he chose to sleep outside, under the stars, and at sunup had vanished. Jordan decided that his suspicions were groundless and resumed his hunt for the cache under the oaks strewn over the flat. A day's strenuous search uncovered nothing. And he decided to transfer his investigations to the narrow canyon in the rear of the cabin.

Night clothed the solitudes. He lay on his bunk, reflectively reviewing progress, when a shrill whinny from the direction of the corral brought him to his feet. Could be the dun had scented a cougar prowling around, he decided, or maybe another horse had wandered into the vicinity. He lifted the stable lamp down from its hook and hit for the corral.

The moon was full, laying a silver sheen on barn and cabin, and etching the surrounding terrain with a black tracery of shadow.

Nothing seemed to be amiss, but the pony was restless, nervously circling the corral. Must be cougar scent, reflected Jordan, and returned to the cabin.

He stepped through the open doorway, set the lamp on the table, whirled at a crisp command—'Hanz up!'

A wiry rider, in ragged range garb, had stepped from behind the open door. Waist high, he held a levelled .45. There was a tautness about the stranger, a wild glare in his pale eyes, that told Jordan he was keyed to killing point.

Promptly, Jordan elevated his arms shoulder high, weighing his unexpected visitor. The intruder was narrow-shouldered, slightly stooped; a shapeless Stetson was yanked over dank black hair. Beard stubbled his jaw and his thin features were wizened and blackened by the sun. His blue shirt was stiff with grime and his discolored levis ripped in a dozen places. Parted in a snarl, his querulous lips quivered and the broken-nailed fingers that grasped the gun reminded Jordan of talons. Edgy as a spitting cat, he registered. This saddle tramp was dangerous, a killer, in a killing mood.

The stranger backheeled and kicked the door shut. 'Drop your gunbelt, easy like,' he directed in high-pitched, nasal tones.

Jordan nodded mutely, backed as though scared, until he stood beyond the table, unbuckled his gunbelt with fumbling fingers. It fell with a flat plunk to the floor.

The stranger moved toward him and Jordan noticed that he limped. 'That dogblasted bronk of yourn kicked me,' he complained.

'Sorry, pard!' Jordan smiled with his lips, but his eyes were cold and wary. 'How come you were fussing around the dun?'

'That snake-eyed broomtail I forked broke a leg. I need a mount.'

'There's one in the corral. Why brace me?'

'Afore I leave I got a debt to pay—for Joe.'

'Joe?' Jordan looked puzzled.

'Joe Leggett, my pard. You turned him over to the law.'

Light broke upon Jordan. So this was Bill Negg, the third member of the hold-up gang, the *hombre* Sheriff Haslipp had warned him about. 'Heck,' he protested, 'Leggett was hellbent to bushwhack me.'

'You had it coming!' shrilled the wizened gunman. 'Jed Harker crossed us. Jed sent you back to grab the train loot. Wal, you ain't never going to get away with it.'

'You got this all wrong, Bill,' declared Jordan earnestly. 'I just bought a half-section. If there's loot around, grab it and vamoose.'

'Quit spilling windies!' snarled the other. His thin features twitched at a twinge of pain. He dropped onto the bench on the further side of the table from Jordan, steadied the pointing gun with an elbow on the table top.

Jordan thought fast. This *hombre* was poisoned with hate and frustration and as dangerous as a diamondback. 'I'll—I'll make a deal,' he quavered.

'So I guessed right,' spat the wizened rider. 'You're sidin' Jed. Wal, mister, it'll sure be a pleasure to watch you kick.'

'Listen!' begged Jordan. 'Harker left the loot cached—in the canyon. I can lead you to it. I'll trade—my life for a quarter-million.'

Negg's features twisted into a pleased grin. He rose awkwardly. 'Hunky-dory! Lead me up canyon. You try any shenanigans, mister, I'll sure as hell smash your spine.'

Jordan dropped his arms and eagerly stepped forward. As he passed the table, he tripped over the gunbelt, staggered, then abruptly galvanized into lightning action. Throwing his body sideways, he sent the table flying. The stable lamp spilled. As it crashed to the ground, the glass funnel shattered and the light was promptly extinguished. At the same instant, Negg's gun spurted red fire. A slug splintered the far wall. By the powderflash, Jordan, prone and rolling, glimpsed his own gunbelt and gathered it in with a sweep of an arm.

Another powderflash illumined the cabin. A bullet bored through the overturned table, not a foot from his head. By then he had slipped his .45 out of leather and, for the first time in many minutes, was conscious of vast relief.

There was silence. Acrid powder fumes filled the darkened cabin and gripped Jordan's throat. Slowly, he began to squirm behind the table, gun in one hand, gunbelt in the other. One of his boots stirred a fragment of broken glass. The tinkle was loud in the tight silence. From the direction of the doorway, a gun flamed again, low down. Without pause, Jordan triggered twice, in return. But a stab of pain across the thick of his right leg, like the sudden application of a redhot branding iron, disturbed his aim. Silently, spread-eagled behind the upturned table, he fingered the leg through his pants and his hand came away sticky wet.

Tight lipped, he waited. It was apparent that one of them, or maybe both, would never leave that cabin alive.

The powdersmoke was suffocating now. He fought an urge to cough. There was no further sound from the doorway but he knew that Negg was crouched there, techy as a teased rattlesnake, gun levelled, seeking a mark.

Groping around cautiously, he found the stable lamp. Gripping it, he began to edge, crabwise, away from the table, inching almost imperceptibly for fear of disturbing more broken glass. Through black darkness, roiling with powder-smoke, he crept toward the bunk. Finally, he came to a sitting position, moving with slow deliberation. The gun in his right hand, stable lamp in his left, he froze, peering into blackness, endeavoring to locate his opponent. A faint, muffled movement from the direction of the doorway reached his ears, as though someone was cramped and cautiously changed position. Without hesitation, he hurled the lamp and dropped flat. With a metallic clang, the lamp hit the door—and thunderous flame stabbed back, once, twice.

Red-tinged through a floating fog, he glimpsed Negg's dark form, crouched low, back against the door. Five shots in all, he registered. If his count was right, the other's gun should be empty. With cool deliberation, he levelled his own .45 and emptied it— throwing hot lead. A long, low groan came to his ears, then silence again.

By feel, he plugged out his empties and inserted fresh loads. Feeling with his feet, he found the overturned table and pushed it. The harsh scraping sound brought no response. Spread-eagled, he lay listening acutely for sound of movement. He thought he heard labored breathing. That was all. For long seconds he waited, nerves taut as fiddle-strings. Then he began easing toward the closed door. Groping ahead, his fingers found a boot. In a flash he flung himself upon a huddled form, but it lay slack and yielding beneath him. He straightened, struck a stinker and stared down in the faint, wavering light. Bill Negg lay in a bloodied heap, his gun slack in lifeless fingers. As the match died, Jordan booted the gun across the floor.

He struck another light, found the battered lamp and tentatively held flame to the wick. It burned, a yellow, smoky flame.

Righting the table, he set the lamp upon it and gave attention to his leg. A slug had gouged the flesh and the gash was bleeding freely. It might have been worse, a heap worse, he considered as he wadded a bandana and secured it over the wound with a strip of towel. Then he hauled Negg's limp form outside. The last of the hold-up gang, he thought, with satisfaction. Tarantulas, every one. Now he could hunt the cache without hindrance.

CHAPTER TEN

Bill Jordan greeted the new day with no pleasure. He felt as ornery as a mule and as sociable as a sore-headed dog. Through the night his injured leg had plagued him. Now it was so stiff that he could scarcely bend it. Furthermore, the unpleasant chore of disposing of Bill Negg's remains awaited him. This last posed a problem. Rightly, he knew he should pack the body to town and make a report of the affray to the sheriff. But he had a hunch that this might lead to complications. Haslipp hadn't been overly friendly. There were no witnesses to back his story that he had killed in self-defense. He had known lawmen who would have clapped a man behind bars for less, far less.

The stiffness of his leg eased a mite after he moved around awhile and a mug of strong coffee brightened his outlook. He decided the corpse was best buried and forgotten. The easiest digging, he reflected, should be down by the creek. Elsewhere the ground was stony and heat-hardened. He found a pick in the barn, selected a spot beyond it, across the creek, which was comparatively free of brush, and began swinging the pick with no enthusiasm.

When finally he had evacuated a six-foot

trench, waist-deep, the sun was arcing overhead, he was begrimed and sweaty, and the gash in his leg burned like slow fire. He cleared out remnants of loose earth with a shovel, dropped it and clambered out. Limping, he hit for the cabin.

A black cloud of flies hovered around the corpse, stiffening now. With distaste, he heaved it over a shoulder, was about to pack it toward the grave when a startled exclamation brought him up short. He swung around, to face Reginald Chumbley. The Englishman's jaw sagged with surprise and his brown eyes focussed the dead man with horrified fascination.

'Ghastly—by love!' ejaculated the tweeded photographer.

Mentally, Jordan cursed the inquisitive newcomer. This was one job he had hoped to finish without interruption. 'Gunfight!' he barked. 'The *hombre* tried to steal my horse.' Then he headed for the creek.

Chumbley trotted beside him, firing questions. Sweating, Jordan silently consigned the Englishman to the same destination he guessed would claim whatever remained of Bill Negg. He dumped the corpse in the trench and a happy thought struck him. 'Reggie!' he directed, 'grab that shovel and cover the gent up.'

'Digging is really not in my line,' protested the Englishman.

93

'Wal, if you want it that way!' said Jordan ominously. He scowled at the ruddy-cheeked man and clapped a hand on his gun butt.

Reggie gaped at the gun, eyed his soft white hands despairingly, and shuffled uncertainly.

'Wal?' drawled Jordan, and pulled the gun.

Reggie hastily grabbed the shovel, lying atop a mound of yellow earth and began vigorously throwing dirt. Jordan sought shade, hunkered, and watched Reginald Chumbley sweat with profound satisfaction.

The rattle of a bit chain beyond the barn brought him to his feet. Who now? he wondered. He was not long in doubt. The two deputies he had encountered when he first rode into town jingled around the angle of the barn.

Jordan mentally castigated himself. Engrossed with the problem of Negg's disposal he had entirely forgotten that the sheriff's office was keeping cases on Harker's place. Through a spyglass, the lawmen had probably watched his every move, eyed him as he packed the corpse from the cabin, and ridden down from their lookout to investigate.

Pecos, the leathery-faced deputy, strode to the edge of the grave and stared down. 'Bill Negg!' he exclaimed. 'I'll be damned!' He eyed Chumbley, fidgeting uneasily, shovel in hand. 'You have a hand in this?'

'Indeed not!' protested the Englishman vehemently. 'I merely dropped in to say "How-

94

do-you-do" and there was this grisly object, staring me in the face.'

'Then how come you're planting Negg?'

'That man,' Chumbley dramatically levelled a forefinger in Jordan's direction, 'forcibly impressed me.'

'He's right,' broke in Jordan, stepping forward. 'He just drifted in. I downed Negg last night, in a gun fight.'

'How come you didn't pack his carcass to town and make a report?' demanded Pecos.

Jordan shrugged.

'Could be murder,' ruminated the deputy. 'Guess we got to take you in, Jordan, f'r questioning. Grab his gun, Sam!'

The other deputy had already stepped up behind Jordan. The rider realized the futility of resistance and made no move as his .45 was lifted out of the holster. Reggie had seized the opportunity to slip away.

Later that day, three men rode into Clearwater. On a pack pony, which the deputies had requisitioned from Irish, the remains of Bill Negg were roped.

Sheriff Haslipp, bulking in his swivel chair, listened to Pecos' report. At its end he eyed the fuming Jordan. 'Wal, what's your story?' he inquired.

In terse sentences the rider told of the disturbance in the corral, the hold-up in his cabin and the fracas that followed.

'No witnesses!' commented the sheriff

thoughtfully.

'Nope,' agreed Jordan, 'nothing more than a bullet burn on my right leg. But you'll recollect, sheriff, you warned me Negg would be deadset to make wormfeed out of me.'

Haslipp chewed his cigar in silence. 'Put the bracelets on him!' he ordered suddenly. Pecos fished out a pair of hand-cuffs from a back pocket, snapped them on the prisoner's wrists.

'Now beat it, boys,' directed the sheriff. 'I crave a few words with this *hombre*—alone.'

When the office door closed behind the two deputies, Haslipp nodded at a chair. 'Rest your legs,' he invited. Wrists manacled, Jordan sat, stiffbacked.

'Guess your luck's running muddy,' began the sheriff, conversationally. 'They fished Harker out of the Rio Grande. I figure you made the lobo talk, then knifed him. After which, you hightail for Copper Valley to grab the loot. You're slick, Jordan, mighty slick.' He paused to light a fresh cigar, then continued, 'You buy a few yearlings and go through the motions of ranching, guessing we might be keeping cases on you. When the time's ripe you lift the loot and vamoose. Joe Leggett almost upset your applecart, and now Bill Negg takes a hand. You been almighty lucky, but your string's done run out.'

'You sound like you been chewing loco weed,' growled Jordan.

Haslipp smiled amicably. 'You asking me to

96

believe that you rode close on six hundred miles to farm a rundown spread? And Jed Harker signed that spread over to you just out of goodwill? Likewise, that you didn't persuade the *hombre* to spill his guts afore you stuck him?' The sheriff's tone became regretful, 'Granted I'm just a dumb lawman, but I sure ain't dumb enough to swallow that.'

'Listen!' put in the prisoner. 'I could no more lay my grubhooks on that loot than I could grab the whiskers of the man in the moon.'

Haslipp just smiled. 'Here's a deal to chew on,' he offered. 'Lead us to the cache and you ride away with a thousand simoleons. You got that coming, for Leggett's apprehension.'

'And leave behind $50,000 bounty money?' inquired Jordan blandly. 'Does that make sense?'

'Quit sunfishing!' grunted the sheriff. 'You won't stick around to collect any bounty, not when you get your hands on that quarter-million. You're in a jackpot, feller. Now you take your choice—a thousand dollars and freedom, or a murder rap.'

'Is self-defense a crime?'

'Would Negg beef you when you're his only link to the loot?'

'He sure did his damnedest!'

'Mebbeso!' The sheriff raised his voice, 'Pecos!'

The leathery-faced deputy stepped through

97

the doorway. 'Book him—suspicion of murder.'

Hunkered in a cell in the basement of the courthouse, Jordan wryly considered his predicament. Lady Luck had sure turned sour on him, he reflected, and he couldn't wholly blame her. If he'd had the savvy to conceal Negg's body in the brush before sunup, he'd never have been in this tight. Even if a jury brought in a verdict of justifiable homicide in Negg's killing, he still faced weeks of confinement, penned up like an animal, awaiting trial before a circuit judge. Gloomily he considered the possibilities, while rats squealed in darkened recesses of the basement and pattered along beams over-head.

Although the sun had not yet set, gloomy obscurity veiled the cells. Below ground level, they received their only light through small barred gratings set high on the walls. Dim in the gloom, ponderous rock pillars criss-crossed the basement, supporting the structure above. Steel barred, the cells lined one wall, each furnished with a straw mattress thrown on a low wooden bench, and a metal bucket. In the end cell, far removed from Jordan, Joe Leggett sulked.

Light had faded to inky darkness when a deputy clomped down a flight of wooden stairs, a stable lamp swinging by its bail from one hand. He hooked the lamp on a peg.

Jordan straightened when he saw that a girl

followed the deputy. In the sickly yellow light, her features were plain. It was Carol Hall. His pulse speeded.

She stepped up to the bars and he advanced to meet her. 'Well, you are in a pickle!' she commented.

Jordan smiled cheerlessly. 'The sheriff got the loco idea I can locate that loot.'

'Sheriff Haslipp is a very astute man,' she said. 'But surely they can't jail you on mere suspicion.'

'The charge is murder!' he told her starkly, and again gave an account of the fracas.

'But there's not a shred of evidence that you didn't act in self-defense,' she protested.

'There's Negg's carcass to prove I killed him,' he replied matter-of-factly. 'Then they caught me planting him—that don't exactly look good.'

'He came to kill you,' she declared, 'just as Leggett did. Those men are wolves, and the sheriff knows it.' She paused. 'Mr. Haslipp has quite a reputation as a poker player. I think he's running a big bluff.'

'Could be,' agreed the prisoner, 'but it sure don't ace me out of here.'

'No local jury would convict you!'

'It's waiting that irks.'

Impulsively, she placed a small hand upon his as he gripped the bars. 'I'm sorry, Bill! You should never have become involved in this horrible business.'

'Guess I'll just have to sweat it out,' he replied, with more disgust than alarm.

'Time's up, Miss Hall!' The jailor emerged from the shadows.

'Good-bye!' she said softly. 'Can I do anything, anything at all?'

'Wal,' the prisoner told her whimsically, 'I sure could use the makin's.'

Carol mounted the stairway at the heels of the plodding jailor. When they stepped into the corridor, he motioned for her to enter the sheriff's office. Sensing what lay ahead, she opened the door, head high.

Bulked in his chair, Haslipp watched her trip toward him, a slim slip of a girl. Irritated speculation lay in his deepset eyes.

Carol Hall was popular. The children idolized her and there wasn't a man around town who wouldn't break a leg to do her a service. Which accounted for the fact, considered the sheriff irascibly, that she'd persuaded that jughead jailor, Bunker, to admit her to the hoosgow during his own brief absence from the office. Not that it caused any harm. He just didn't stomach seeing a real nice girl getting mixed up with a no-good, cold-blooded gunwolf. Why in creation, he wondered morosely, did the most attractive girl around, who could have brought a dozen eligible young fellows arunnin' at the crook of a finger, have to tangle with a chunk of jail bait?

'You wanted to see me, Sheriff?' inquired Carol lightly, perching upon a chair.

'So I ain't "Hank" to you no more?' barked Haslipp.

'Not officially, particularly when you are practically frothing at the mouth,' she smiled.

The sheriff gulped and modified his tone. 'What in thunder you got in common with that no-good border buzzard we picked up?'

'He's a neighbor!' she retorted sweetly.

'Neighbor!' snorted Haslipp. 'You know what brought the lobo to Harker's place? Loot! Jordan's a murdering polecat, a snakeblooded killer, a fiddlefooted coyote.'

The girl tensed. 'And upon what facts do you base these assumptions?'

'Heck, he knifed Jed Harker in the back, salivated Negg and winged a Turtle puncher.'

'I know nothing about this alleged knifing,' she replied unconcernedly, 'but I do know he killed Bill Negg in self-defense. As for the puncher, Buck Burdock and his bullies have been harassing the small ranchers as long as I can remember.'

'So you swallowed Jordan's story—hook, line and sinker,' grunted Haslipp, with disgust.

'Bill Jordan is certainly not the type who would knife a man in the back!'

The sheriff changed his tactics. 'Listen, Carol,' he begged, 'I've known you since you were knee-high. You've never been outside this valley, you just don't savvy bad actors.

101

Jordan is pizon. Don't let the sidewinder buffalo you.'

'Jordan has made no attempt to buffalo me, as you term it,' she replied calmly. 'I think he is unjustly accused and I intend to stand by him.'

'Folks'll talk if you hang around that gunslick,' warned the sheriff ominously. 'You wouldn't want your good name dragged in the dirt, now, would you, Carol, being the school ma'am?'

The girl tossed her head. 'I am free, white and practically twenty-one. The school trustees do not select my friends. As for talk!' She raised her shoulders disdainfully.

Haslipp gave up. He should have known, he thought with disgust. No sane man ever tried to argue with a woman.

'Jordan got just one friend,' he rumbled, 'his gun. No more visits!'

'Very good, Sheriff!' She rose. At the door, she turned and inquired meekly, 'Would it rock the pillars of justice if I sent Jordan some tobacco and cigarette papers?'

Haslipp could do no more than splutter.

CHAPTER ELEVEN

Days dragged for the prisoner. Days penned in the stale stench of the courthouse basement, days that would have been unendurable but that every morning on his tin breakfast tray there lay a small sack of tobacco, a book of papers and a block of matches. Invariably, tight-folded and thrust way down in the tobacco, came a cheerful note from Carol Hall, neatly inscribed upon thin tissue.

One mid-morning, as he hunkered morosely and watched the rats scampering through the shadows, the unexpected occurred. The stolid Bunker trudged down the creaking stair-way, unlocked the cell gate and swung it open. 'Beat it!' he grunted.

'You funnin'?' breathed the prisoner. incredulously, as he came slowly to his feet.

'Sheriff's orders,' returned the jailor. 'Collect your hardware and belongings in the office.'

Scarce believing his good fortune, Jordan followed Bunker's blocky form upstairs. When he strode into the sheriff's office he blinked. Nearby the sheriff, who sat watching him poker-faced, stood a gaunt, rawboned figure with a bushy black beard, arrayed in a rusty frock coat.

'You aceing me out of here?' he demanded

of Paul.

'The arm of the Lord is strong,' boomed the Preacher. 'He dispenseth justice and mercy, even to the most miserable sinner. A wrong is righted.'

'Wal, I'm sure putting up no argument,' declared Jordan. He buckled on his gunbelt and stuffed a long envelope containing jackknife, loose coin, wallet and other personal belongings, into a pants pocket. Then he eyed Haslipp, 'I'm sure thanking you, Sheriff.'

'Thank the Preacher!' snapped the lawman. 'He saved your neck. But you'll be back!'

'Don't gamble on it!' said Jordan shortly.

Paul pacing behind him, the newly-released prisoner strode down the corridor. At the head of the outside steps he paused, inhaling deeply. 'That air sure tastes good, after a stinking cell,' he declared.

'A worthy man would go down on his knees and offer thanks for deliverance,' reproved Paul.

'I ain't that worthy,' grinned Jordan. 'Tell me, how did you rope and hogtie that stiff-necked old son inside?'

'Possess your soul with patience and all shall be made plain, saith the Lord,' boomed Paul. His voice dropped to the conversational, 'Right now we need a shotgun and a coil of bailing wire, sixteen gauge.'

'We need—what?' almost gasped Jordan.

The Preacher's piercing eyes fixed him. 'A

fool when he holds his peace is counted wise,' he roared. 'Get thee to the Mercantile Store, and forget not shells. An empty gun is as useless as an empty head.'

With no more argument, Jordan plowed through the dust across the street and made the necessary purchases.

Later, as the pair followed the river trail, beating up valley, Paul astride his mule and Jordan forking the dun, the Preacher matter-of-factly related that he had felt an urge to ride back to Harker's the night of the fracas. 'The finger of the Lord nudged me,' he explained. Approaching the cabin, he saw Jordan step out with a stable lamp and cross to the corral, and was amazed to see another man slink into the cabin. Forthwith, he had slipped off his mount and ghosted close.

When Jordan returned, he heard Negg's challenge. Then the door banged shut, the light blinked out and shooting began. He merely sat on the bench outside and awaited developments. After awhile, Negg's lifeless body was pitched out. Deciding it was strictly a personal feud, he rode away, and had only learned of Jordan's arrest on a murder charge from a chance remark, caught when he dropped into a bunk-house for supper. Thereupon he had headed for Clearwater and braced the sheriff.

Thankful though he was for release, Jordan couldn't but reflect upon the attention

Harker's place had for all. 'What really had brought the Preacher back to the cabin after dark? How come the wide-eyed Reginald Chumbley just chanced to be around when he was disposing of Negg's remains. Without a mount, too! Aloud, he said feelingly, 'Wal, you sure aced me out of a tight.'

'Do unto others as you would have others do unto you,' intoned Paul.

An angry exclamation left Jordan's lips when they finally came in sight of Harker's place. Again, the flat was thick with Turtle cows. Along the river front, the three-strand barbed wire fence upon which he had expended so much sweat had been destroyed. Only the posts remained, a long row of forlorn sentinels; the cut wire was coiled in ragged tangles around them.

Paul followed the direction of his glance. 'Barbed wire is an abomination in the eyes of Buck Burdock,' he commented. 'On the morrow we will restring the fence.'

'So the Turtle can cut it again!'

The Preacher's grim lips curled in a smile. 'That is a consummation devoutly to be hoped, brother '

Jordan's forehead wrinkled. He guessed Paul's complacence was somehow linked up with the shotgun and the coil of smooth wire.

There was an extra spool of barbed wire in the barn. At sunup the pair got busy untangling and restringing wire, mending, straightening, tacking. When they were through, there remained a tangle of shorter lengths, discarded. These Paul insisted upon packing across the river.

A profusion of brush clothed the further bank, high as a pony's belly. Under Paul's direction, Jordan dragged the coiled, barbed lengths into it, dumping them indiscriminately in a steel-thorned tangle. It was laborious, lacerating work. The barbs tore his garb, cut his hands, coiled around his legs. But he made no complaint. Light was beginning to dawn.

Finally, the Preacher drove two stout posts down; they protruded a scant two feet above ground, one on the bank and the other a hundred paces inland. Between them he strung a single taut strand of smooth bailing wire, and he affixed the shotgun in such a position that a pull on the wire would trip its trigger. This done, he beat the dust from his shabby pants and stood stroking his sable beard, plainly well pleased.

'Is the mystery made plain?' he inquired.

Jordan smiled broadly as he mopped his damp brow. 'I guess so,' he admitted. 'You're uncommon slick for a preacher. Sure as hell the Turtle boys will come ariding to cut my wire again after sundown. The barbs of the loose wire lacing the brush will play heck with their ponies and when they hit the strand of bailing wire, as they will, the shotgun blast will maybe spread more hell.'

107

Paul nodded benignly. 'The wicked shall fall by his own wickedness,' he declared sonorously.

That night a shotgun blast across river awakened Jordan. The Preacher's mule was in the corral but his master lay somewhere out in the brush.

Jordan yanked on his boots, grabbed the Winchester and ran outside. Mist veiled the river and blotted out sight of the further bank, but through it came the squeals of affrighted ponies, thrashing madly around in the brush, and the yelling of angry men. Gradually, the turmoil died. At daybreak, the wire fence was untouched.

'I gamble,' Jordan told the Preacher, as they demolished a stack of flapjacks at breakfast, 'the Turtle bunch is almighty busy, doctoring wire cuts.'

'The way of the transgressor is hard,' rumbled Paul, and spilled more syrup over his flapjacks. 'Alas, being hot-headed, they will return—and not with wirecutters.' Jordan ate in silence. The words seemed ominous.

Shortly before noon, a red-shirted rider came jogging down river, forking a calico pony.

'Irish,' Jordan told the Preacher, 'my neighbor.'

'We have met,' Paul's voice held disapproval. 'He hath set up false idols and he mocks the Word.'

The lanky breed checked his pony a few paces from the pair and weighed them with calm blue eyes, as they sat on the bench. Finally, he commented, 'You gents sure raised a ruckus last night.'

'I reckon you're barking up the wrong tree,' averred Jordan, straight-faced. 'Me and the Preacher were as peaceful as two puppies on a warm brick.'

'Then someone's chewing locoweed,' retorted Irish and stepped off the pony. 'I rode over to the Turtle to top off some bronks for Buck. The Old Man's mad enough to eat the devil with his horns on. Six Turtle ponies are wire-cut, had to shoot one. Two gents were thrown, one busted a laig. All on account some son-of-a-gun set trip wires.' He jackknifed his beanpole form onto the bench beside Jordan. 'There'll be hell to pay.'

'Such as?' inquired Jordan.

'Buck announced his intention of shooting you so full of holes you won't hold hay. I reckon you can expect the visiting delegates around sunup.'

'I sure thank you for the tip-off.'

For minutes the three sat in silent contemplation.

'Guess you'll head for the hills,' contributed Irish, at length.

'I figure the Turtle boys are entitled to a reception committee,' decided Jordan slowly.

'You hungry for a headstone?'

'Nope, just obstinate,' smiled Jordan.

'The way of a fool is past understanding,' intoned the Preacher.

'You'll last as long as a wax cat in hell, you stick around,' objected Irish. 'An hour's ride and you're buried in the Bad Lands. I kin lead you to a hideaway where a troop of U.S. Cavalry would never flush you out.'

'It is even better to get wisdom than gold, brother,' intoned Paul. 'Head for the hills!'

'I got different ideas,' insisted Jordan stubbornly. 'I'd stake my saddle against a beer check that the Law's keeping cases on me right now.' He told of the giveaway flash on the hillside. 'Dead,' he concluded, 'I'm buzzard bait. Alive, the sheriff figures I'm his last bet to locate that looted gold.'

'So you figure the Law will ace you out of the jackpot?' commented Irish.

'I'm gambling on it.' When the Turtle starts throwing lead, the lookout hightails for town and a sheriff's posse fogs out.'

'The love of money is the root of all evil,' droned Paul. 'So the gold lies hereabouts, brother?'

'Your guess is as good as mine,' threw back Jordan.

'Harker sure enough cached it hereabouts,' contributed Irish. He came to his feet, 'Wal, this ain't my fight. Guess I'll light a shuck.' He eyed the Preacher, 'You sticking around to swallow lead?'

'I will meditate on the matter, brother,' replied Paul calmly. 'The Lord said, "succor the oppressed."'

Watching the breed as his pony jogged riverward, Jordan considered the saloon man's warning that Irish might be tied up with the gang. If Jed Harker was his cousin, it was a sure thing that blood was thicker than water. Yet Irish had warned him, and offered to lead him to a hideaway. Could be, considered the rider, Irish considered him more useful alive than dead.

A molten ball, the sun climbed the heavens. Jordan filled both buckets with water and set them in the cabin, then waded across river and brought back the shotgun. He needed all the fire power he could muster, he reflected, if he was to hold off the Turtle bunch long enough for Haslipp to take a hand.

The Preacher seemed in no hurry to move. With sundown, Jordan prodded him. 'I figure you should make tracks, Preacher,' he said. 'The Turtle boys are liable to drop by any time now.'

'The wicked flee when no man pursueth,' chided Paul. 'I am encompassed by the armor of righteousness, no harm shall befall the godly.'

'I sure wouldn't bank on it,' threw back Jordan. 'Slugs ain't chooscy.' He stood surveying the cabin. It was constructed of hewn timbers, now grayed and sun-dried,

111

chinked with crumbling mud. Then he stepped to a window and eyed the terrain around. In every direction, for at least fifty paces, there was a clear field of fire, and little cover. With luck, he decided, a man could hold that cabin at long odds—as long as daylight lasted. With darkness, it would be a different story. He could only hope that Burdock, confident of easy victory, would attack at dawn, as Irish had forecast.

When the stars pricked through the darkening heavens and Paul still showed no inclination to pull out, Jordan made another attempt at persuasion. The Preacher merely ignored him. Then an idea struck Jordan, who had little liking to involve another man in his troubles, particularly since he considered himself deeply indebted to that man. 'I get it now,' he commented. 'You got a yen to lay your grubhooks on that quarter-million cartwheels. You figure I'll stop a slug and spill my guts afore I check out.'

'Oh, wretched ingrate!' roared Paul. 'Is this my reward for snatching you from a cell, for siding you against the powers of evil? Shame, doubter, you will surely be consigned to the nethermost depths of hell.' Then he stroked his beard and smiled. His voice dropped to the normal. 'That was a good try, Jordan, but I'm sticking around to side you.' That night, for the first time, he slept in the cabin, stretched out on the packed earth floor.

Before the mist that clung to the river evaporated, Jordan was up and around. Above, the stars were fading. Tenuous fingers of light groped across the heavens. Eastward, the tortured outline of the Black Kaweahs showed somber against a pallid forecast of dawn.

Paul heaved, was wide awake, and came to his feet like a great hairy bear. 'Brother,' he boomed, 'before the sun sets your soul may wing its way to Purgatory. On your knees, sinner, to pray forgiveness for your many misdeeds.'

'I just ain't in practice, Preacher,' grunted the rider, busy starting a fire in the stove.

'Then go to hell!' retorted Paul, and the tone in which he said it, considered Jordan, was most unclerical.

They were sipping scalding coffee when Paul tensed. 'Ponies,' he said shortly, 'cantering.' Three quick steps and Jordan was at a window. From out of the river mist a cavalcade emerged. Same number as before, he noted, tallying seven riders. But this time they made no attempt to approach the cabin. Circling, they swept out of sight before the barn and were hidden by the brush that bunched along the creek.

There were two small windows in the cabin, one front and the other centering the rear wall. This limited the defenders' field of vision. But, shortly after, from the rear window,

Jordan glimpsed several punchers afoot, slipping through the brush. Their intent was plain—surround the cabin.

Laconically, he announced, 'We're bottled up!' The Preacher nodded, set his mug down and reached for the shotgun. Actually, Jordan knew, the scattergun was useless except at close range. For the moment, their only effective weapon was his Winchester.

He levered a shell into the breach, and resumed his place at the window, standing obliquely to one side.

With a sharp crackle, the window shattered. Broken glass tinkled down onto the dirt floor and a slug thudded into the opposite wall. Then the remaining window exploded into fragments. Lead began whining. through the two window frames, now edged with jagged fragments of glass. The stovepipe came down with a resounding clang. Drifting smoke set the two men, who had thrown themselves flat, coughing. Jordan crawled over to the stove, shook the remnants of the fire into the ash box and smothered the glowing embers. A breeze, fragrant with sage scent, made a welcome draft through the broken windows. Gradually, the air cleared.

After the initial fusillade, the mingling crackle of gunfire died down, succeeded by desultory shooting. Jordan snapped open his jackknife, slid behind the stove and began digging out the mud chinking between two logs, to form a peephole. Otherwise, he reflected, that side was blind. An attacker could creep right up to the cabin unseen.

The Preacher, grasping his intent, got busy at the other end of the cabin, over the bunk.

When a field of view was opened up on all sides, Jordan took up post again beside the window. Regularly, like a buzzing hornet, a bullet droned through the glassless frame, within a foot of his nose. And it always came from the same direction. Searching for sign of the marksman, Jordan finally glimpsed a faint cloud of powdersmoke that persistently drifted above a tumbled heap of rock, crowned by a stunted oak. As he watched, another slug whipped through the window and the gunsmoke thickened.

So that was the location of the gun-slinging hornet, he reflected. At the distance, however, details were indistinct and nothing more than the smoke haze betrayed the position of the marksman.

'If I had a spyglass,' he grumbled, 'I could get me a scalp.'

Without a word, Paul dug inside his coat tails and brought out a small pair of leather-covered field glasses. Joyously, Jordan focussed upon the heap of rock.

Almost immediately he found what he sought. Plain in the lens was the outline of a man's upper body, as he crouched behind the boulder upon which his rifle rested. Lack of return fire had made him careless—head and shoulders were plainly exposed.

Marking the spot carefully, Jordan set the glasses aside, stepped back and rested the muzzle of his Winchester on the window ledge. Slowly he lined on his mark, squeezed the trigger—and grabbed for the glasses. Dust rose amid the boulders. A shirted form dabbed in and out of view, thrashing convulsively.

'Hit the bull's-eye!' announced Jordan with satisfaction.

'He that killeth by the sword will likely die by the sword, brother,' intoned Paul. 'Stand clear of the window!'

The value of his advice quickly became evident. Gunfire exploded afresh, lashing the cabin with lead.

Hours crawled, the heat built up, and intermittent gunfire reverberated through the hills. But the defenders never caught a glimpse of another attacker. 'I guess,' said Jordan, 'they're waiting for nightfall afore they close in.'

Paul took a long drink from the dipper. 'Pray for relief before sundown, brother,' he advised. 'A little brush heaped against this sun-dried cabin, a match, and—'

'Hell fire!' put in Jordan dryly.

It wasn't a pleasant thought and it lingered persistently in his mind as the hours crept by and the sun dropped down. Finally shadows began to wreathe the hills. Maybe his guess that Sheriff Haslipp still kept a deputy on lookout had been wrong. What if he was betting on a busted flush?

CHAPTER TWELVE

Staring out at the slowly darkening terrain through the shattered window, Jordan considered their predicament. He'd gambled that the Law would ace him out of this tight and it seemed he'd bet on a dead horse. Come night, the Turtle boys could crawl close and fire the cabin. With its sun-dried timbers, the place would flare like a torch.

Then a feeling gripped him that something was amiss. It was minutes before he could pinpoint the discrepancy. Their attackers had quit throwing lead. He turned in the direction of the Preacher, a shadow in the darkened cabin, and relayed the information. 'Guess the boys are cooking up a fourth of July celebration,' he concluded wryly.

'Betsy will have her say in that,' rumbled Paul, slapping the fat barrel of the shotgun. 'Eighteen pellets to the shell. That is a powerful deterrent, brother.'

'Strong medicine,' agreed Jordan, 'but it just ain't strong enough.'

Both men prowled restlessly around the cabin, peering out, searching for sign of movement in the gloom that shrouded them. Then the thud of shod hooves was plain, slowly dying with distance.

'I'll be damned!' exclaimed Jordan, as the

significance of the sound struck him. 'You hear that, Preacher?'

'The Lord hath delivered us out of the hands of our enemies,' intoned Paul. 'He hath wrought a miracle.'

'Miracle heck!' retorted Jordan, listening intently at a window. 'We drew aces—the sheriff's posse!'

The jingle of bit chains came to their ears, and a solid block of riders, vague in the dying light, jogged toward the cabin across the flat.

Jordan hurriedly unbarred the door and stepped outside, Winchester ready. The riders checked and sat their saddles, a dark smudge against the night. One eased his mount ahead and the sheriff's hail reached Jordan's ears, 'You got trouble?'

'Plenty!' returned the rider. 'The Turtle been blasting us since sunup. They just beat it.'

'Us?'

'Me and the Preacher.'

Haslipp rode closer and swung out of leather. 'You'll wallow in trouble 'til you deliver that loot,' he barked. 'In the name of creation, why don't you wise up?'

Paul's rawboned form appeared in the doorway. 'He who worships Mammon bows down to false gods,' he droned. 'Better a pure heart, brother, than a lead slug.'

'If I could get my grubhooks on that cache,' snapped Jordan, 'you figure I'd stick around here?'

'Nope,' grunted the sheriff, 'you'd high-tail, pronto. Could be you're all primed to high-tail.'

Jordan raised his shoulders stoically, realizing the futility of argument. The sheriff, it was plain, would never believe that he hadn't the faintest notion where the spoils from the train robbery were cached.

Haslipp turned toward the bunched riders. 'Ease your saddles and rest awhile, boys,' he directed. Jordan lit the battered oil lamp and called the lawman's attention to the shattered windows and bullet-pocked walls. 'You going to allow Buck Burdock to get away with this?' he demanded. 'What right has that big buffalo got to shoot up my place?'

It was the sheriff's turn to button up. It wasn't easy to explain that he was an elected official. The cattlemen stuck together. If he sided a homesteader against one of them he'd throw a bucketful of votes out of the window. With an election coming up in less than three months he would be as good as out of office. Already his failure to recover the train loot had stirred talk. It was whispered around that he had been toting the badge too long, that maybe the time was ripe to put him out to pasture. That the office called for a younger and more vigorous man. Haslipp had his problems, too.

When, finally, the posse jingled away, Jordan and the Preacher sat on the bench, rolled smokes and eyed a smother of stars. After being penned up in the stifling heat of the closed cabin all day, it was a relief to relax and breathe the cool night air.

'You know,' commented Jordan, 'a fat chunk of loot sure brings the buzzards afluttering. First there was Leggett, then his pard Negg. Irish had blood ties with Harker and I gamble he's got an eye on the jackpot, too. Then that Limey, Reginald Chumbley—'

'Alias Five-ace Freddy,' put in Paul. 'Run out of Kansas City. Blossomed again in El Paso. There, I believe the tag was Whitechapel Willy. He never could resist the lure of easy money.' The Preacher sighed, 'A devious soul, beyond redemption.'

'So the Limey's on the trail of the quarter-million, too,' murmured Jordan. He eyed Paul, 'I ain't too sure of you!'

'Put not your trust in riches,' droned the Preacher. 'My wealth is eternal, brother. Store up your treasure in heaven, saith the Lord.'

'You sure changed plenty since you helled around Texas!'

'I have seen the Light,' replied Paul simply.

With sunup, Jordan found that the Preacher had vanished. The bearded man was hard to figure. He was apparently pursuing the pathway of salvation just as vigorously as he had once followed that of crime. You had to hand it to Paul, reflected the rider. When the bearded man set a course, he stuck to it, and

121

fear was not in his vocabulary. Then he gave thought to his own affairs. It was getting too warm around Harker's place to be comfortable. If he didn't get busy and locate that quarter-million he'd likely never survive to enjoy its fruits. Maybe he should explore the canyon.

After eating, he headed toward the scattered scrub oak in the rear of the cabin, breasted the brush that had shielded him from Leggett's lead, worked upward as the terrain funnelled into the canyon. Here steep slopes walled him in on either side, veined by ledges and crusted with eroding rock.

He picked his laborious way through an ancient water course, now choked with boulders that had cascaded down the slopes. Steadily, he scrambled higher and higher. There was little vegetation in the bouldery wash, beyond an occasional clump of stately bear grass and nests of prickly ocatillo.

Breathing hard from his exertions, he slipped and slithered over the welter of loose rock, the ascent growing steeper as the confining walls closed in. Finally, the futility of his search struck him. He stopped, chest heaving. There were a hundred, a thousand, spots in that canyon where a man could conceal loot. Searchers could spend a year, ten years, fruitlessly ferreting among the rocks. If Harker had cached that quarter-million in the canyon, he decided wryly, it was cached for keeps.

Rather than scramble down again over the bouldery bed, he angled across the hillside, clambering from ledge to ledge. Finally, he reached a level, brush-cluttered bench. Dust-smothered, shins and elbows sore from contact with rough rock, he paused. Way below lay the 'V' of the canyon, beyond it the cabin, toylike, nestling on the flat, with the river, sparkling in the sun, coiling in the background. He was about to move ahead again when he checked, blinking with surprise. Set close to a gnarled old juniper was a long, slim object, draped with a dark cloth and affixed atop a metal tripod.

Cautiously, he glanced around, a hand creeping toward his gun. But the bench was apparently deserted, except for himself. Then he stepped up to the tripod and flicked the cloth off. A handsome telescope was revealed. When he bent and glanced through the eyepiece he was not surprised to discover that it was focussed on the cabin. Every detail distinct, the building was seemingly not a stone's throw distant.

So not only was there a sheriff's deputy keeping cases on him from the hills to the east, he reflected, but here was another *hombre* interested in his movements. For a space, he stood rasping his chin, then he carefully draped the telescope again. Moving across the bench, he found a convenient low-spreading mesquite, dropped down behind it and composed himself to wait.

Scarcely had he settled down, resigned to a long vigil, when the clatter of a carelessly kicked pebble reached his ears. Alert, he waited, bellied beneath the mesquite.

Reginald Chumbley sauntered into view.

The Englishman had discarded his white silk shirt and cream Stetson for more somber and less conspicuous garb. A gray flannel shirt draped his shoulders and he wore blue denims, stiff from the store shelf. An old felt hat, dilapidated enough to be a Cy Plummer discard and plainly too large, was yanked down to his ears.

Whistling off key, he removed the cloth from the telescope and folded it carefully. Then he glanced casually through the eyepiece, turned away, spread the cloth over a flat boulder, seated himself and pulled out pipe and tobacco.

Behind him, Jordan rose silently and eased across the bench. But his movements, cautious as they were, brought Chumbley's head around with quick alarm. At sight of Jordan, stalking toward him, his right hand jerked impulsively inside his shirt. But Jordan's gun snaked out. 'Yank that hideaway,' he yelled, 'and you're dead meat.'

Reluctantly, the Englishman's hand dropped away.

Jordan strode up. His left hand dabbed under the gray shirt and came out grasping a snub-nosed .41 derringer.

'So you detest lethal weapons!' he drawled, and stuck the stubby gun into a pants pocket. 'Now, Mister Chumbley, start talking, and talk fast. How come you're keeping cases on me?'

The ruddy-faced photographer had recovered his aplomb. His brow wrinkled, 'I really don't grasp the allusion, old chap.'

'Quit acting dumb!' growled Jordan and nodded at the telescope.

'Oh that!' Chumbley smiled guilelessly. 'I spend hours surveying wild life, watching the birds. Why, only yesterday—'

'Quit dribbling!' cut in Jordan wearily. 'That telescope is focussed on my cabin. That's how come you saw me planting Negg and dropped down to investigate,'

'Possibly!' agreed the Englishman blandly. 'I assure you, however, the whole thing was purely accidental.'

'You were spying!'

'I resent the aspersion!' bristled Chumbley.

'I'll make it plain, Whitechapel Willy,' barked Jordan. 'You got a yen to collect a little easy money. Wal, Willy, your collecting days are over. March!'

'Ridiculous!' fumed the other. He bent and picked up pipe and tobacco pouch, which he had dropped. Tailed by the rider, he began to trudge across the bench.

When they reached the cabin, Irish's beanpole form was jackknifed on the bench.

Inscrutable, his blue eyes dwelt on Jordan. 'Luck sure sits on your shirttail,' he commented. 'Figured you'd be twanging a harp.' His gaze shifted to Chumbley.

'This gent been bird-watching,' explained Jordan. 'I'm the bird!'

'Merely an unfortunate misunderstanding,' protested the Englishman with dignity.

Jordan ignored him. 'In the U.S. Cavalry,' he inquired of the former scout, 'just how would they handle a spy?'

'Shoot the bustard!' replied Irish expressionlessly.

'A sensible idea!' approved Jordan. He turned to Chumbley, 'Head for the barn yonder!'

The Englishman seemed about to speak, but locked his lips. Dogged by Jordan, Irish trailing in their wake, he headed for the barn. They passed the barn and crossed the creek, beyond which the grave excavated for Negg's remains still gaped, ringed by mounds of yellow earth. A long-handled shovel lay where it had been dropped.

Jordan looked the grave over. 'Guess there's a little loose dirt needs to be cleaned out,' he decided. 'Grab the shovel and get busy, Reggie!'

'This farce has gone far enough!' declared the Englishman. Sweat had begun to bead upon his brow.

'If you think I'm fooling, you're loco,'

drawled Jordan. He fingered the butt of his .45. 'You crave to be planted proper, or do I drop you right now?'

Chambley's despairing glance went to Irish. 'Are you going to stand by and watch him murder me?' he demanded, a quaver in his voice.

The tall breed gave no sign that he heard, simply stood still as a statue, only his eyes moved, as they swivelled from Jordan to the perspiring Englishman.

'You'll hang!' Chumbley told Jordan tonelessly.

'Who's to testify?' drawled the rider. He turned toward Irish and dropped an eyelid. 'You with me, pard?'

' 'Til hell freezes over!' the breed assured him, features expressionless.

'Hear that, Reggie?' inquired Jordan. 'Now get busy, I sure hate a messy killing.'

Leadenly, Chumbley walked to the edge of the grave, bent stiffly and picked up the shovel, turned and hurled it at his tormentor. Jordan, watching alertly, ducked to one side.

With hopeless mien, the Englishman slid down into the grave. Jordan picked up the shovel and tossed it into the excavation. Listlessly, Chumbley began to throw dirt.

Rolling a smoke, Jordan stood watching the chubby man lifelessly wielding the shovel. He was determined to scare the lights out of Chumbley so thoroughly that the confidence man, alias photographer, would never venture near the Harker place again.

Then, as the Englishman glanced up, Jordan was amazed to see the dull hopelessness in his eyes abruptly vanish, succeeded by a quick flash of relief and surprise. Before he could figure the reason, something hard and heavy slammed down on the back of his head like a sledge hammer. A black roaring vortex engulfed his consciousness. His knees crumbled. He collapsed limply on the brink of the grave and lay unmoving.

'Excellent!' shouted Chumbley, his voice shrill with relief. He dropped the shovel and began to scramble out of the hole. The yielding earth at the edge collapsed and he fell back.

Irish, standing behind Jordan's inert form, tossed the smooth chunk of rock he was holding aside. Then his right hand dabbed down and he slipped the unconscious man's .45 out of the holster.

Chumbley, plastered red with earth, scrambled to his feet. 'Give me a hand!' he panted, reaching toward Irish.

'Hold it!' The breed's voice was toneless.

The Englishman stared up at the tall, saturnine figure. Protest died on his lips, his jaw slackened. His features a contorted mask of amazement, he stood gaping at the black muzzle of the .45.

128

The gun roared. Impact of the heavy slug pounded Chumbley backward. He staggered, fell on his back, eyes still staring in startled disbelief. A brown stain was fast-spreading over the front of his gray shirt. His limbs quivered, his eyes closed; then he was still.

Unhurriedly, Irish returned the gun to Jordan's holster. He pulled a leather twang from a pants pocket, yanked the unconscious rider's arms behind him and lashed his wrists. Then he hunkered, his brown fingers fashioning a quirly.

Jordan struggled out of the depths of a dark abyss. As consciousness flowed back, he blinked, screwing his eyes shut against the flood of bright sunlight. He moaned as he tried to move his head and an agonizing spasm shot down his spine. His brain fuzzy, pain-wracked and bewildered, he fought to clarify his thoughts.

Finally, he struggled to a sitting position, stared down incredulously at Chumbley's bloodied form and glanced dazedly around. A shadow fell across him as Irish rose. Jordan painfully levered his head up to focus the tall form. 'You did—that?' he croaked.

Without replying, Irish strode away in the direction of the barn. Left alone, Jordan flopped down onto his back again and fervently wished that his head would stop pounding for just one minute so that he could think straight. As he lay lax, the waves of pain began to subside, succeeded by a dull, throbbing headache. Recollection seeped back—the amazement in Chumbley's eyes, the crash on his head. It was plain now. Irish had downed him from behind and then plugged the Englishman. Why?

The question seemed unanswerable.

CHAPTER THIRTEEN

After a while, Jordan heard a shot from the direction of the river. Hoofbeats brought him to a sitting position again. He strove to free his arms; but the rawhide only cut deeper into his wrists. Irish came into view. Heaped across his pony's withers, and flopping on either side like a huge sack, were the folds of a wet hide. Meaning of the shot became plain; the breed had shot a steer and skinned it.

Irish dumped the hide, ground-hitched his pony and hunkered close by the prisoner. His eyes, blue as bottle glass and as hard, dwelt on Jordan.

'So you're chasing Harker's gold, too!' commented Jordan. 'Figure to dump me with Chumbley and cut down the competition?'

'Mebbee!' replied the breed.

'Wal, get it over!'

'Mebbe you'll live.'

'What's the deal?' He didn't need ask, thought Jordan. It was plain enough, now that Irish had shown his hand. Like the sheriff, he figured that Harker had sent him back to pick up the loot. A killing didn't amount to much where a quarter-million was at stake, but Irish was too smart to kill a man who he thought could lead him to the loot. Carelessness again, considered Jordan gloomily. He had guessed the breed might butt in and he should have watched him. But who would figure on anything as sudden and ruthless as this?

The breed was talking again. 'You made a deal with Jed Harker,' he accused, in his deep, unhurried voice. 'You dig up the loot—you two split. But the sheriff watched. The Preacher watched. Chumbley,' he nodded carelessly in the direction of the Englishman's limp form, 'he watched. I watch, too. So you wait. Maybe you wait too long. Buck Burdock, he will kill you, sure. Then the loot is lost. You better talk—now.'

'You got it wrong—I got nothing to talk about,' protested Jordan.

'We shall see!' returned Irish.

He rose and Jordan watched, puzzled, as he began to lay out the fresh hide. Then understanding came to the prisoner and his intestines shrank and knotted as he realized the breed's intent.

The hide spread, Irish gathered up Jordan as casually as if he was handling a sack of wheat and dumped him at one end. He tucked the edge of the hide around the prisoner's recumbent form and slowly began to roll his body over and over, wrapping it in hide, as though he were rolling up a carpet. Finally, he cut two long strips of hide with his knife and secured the unwieldy bundle, with Jordan in its center.

Enveloped in the stinking, clinging folds,

132

only his head protruding, the helpless prisoner could only glare at his captor. As an afterthought, the breed yanked off Jordan's bandana and tied it securely over his mouth.

Apparently well satisfied with his job, he stood gazing down. 'You know cowhide?' he queried. 'It shrinks as it dries, and it dries quick in the sun. The Apache, they tie a strip around a prisoner's head. It get tighter, tighter, it bursts his skull and squeezes out his brains like a busted egg.' He eyed the sun, just past meridian. 'I go to the cabin, come back at sundown. Then you talk—plenty!' With that, he stalked over to his pony, swung across it and moved away. The prisoner heard the pony splash across the creek. Then all was still.

Left in the broiling sun, Jordan fought recurrent waves of nausea and endeavored desperately to marshal his thoughts. Too well, he knew the crushing effect of the fresh hide when it shrank in the drying process. He'd seen the mashed remnants of a man who had been lashed in a cowhide by vaqueros in revenge for a knifing and the remembrance still sickened his stomach.

Fighting incipient panic, he considered his chances. They seemed slim. There was only the Preacher, but if Paul should make one of his unexpected visits to the cabin Irish would be there to sidetrack him with a plausible story. Something began crawling up one leg. Suddenly, a paroxysm of terror seized him. He

133

heaved and kicked, struggling frantically to loose his trussed wrists and throw off the suffocating folds of wet hide. But the effort did no more than leave him exhausted, sweat-soaked and shaking. Teeth gritted, he mastered an impulse to shriek, scream through his gag, to attract the attention of the breed somehow and beg Irish to mercifully shoot him, anything to escape the slow torture of a strangling death as the hide shrank, and crushed chest, ribs, hips into pulp.

The aching complaint of his head forgotten, he fought for self-control and reason. Finally, the hysteria conquered, he raised his head and looked around. Behind him lay the wall of brush that marked the creek bank. Beyond it rose the bulk of the barn. Close by, mounds of earth showed the outline of the grave. Riverward, his view was blocked by clumped brush, and up creek the terrain rose to flow into a rounded hill.

He glanced down at the unwieldy bulk of the hide that enveloped him and horror chilled him. The hide was black with crawling ants, attracted by the stench of the raw flesh adhering to its underside. Long before sundown they would be swarming over his body, burrow into eyes, nose, ears. Helpless to resist, the torture would convert him into a raving maniac. When the breed returned he would find his victim eaten alive.

Helplessly trussed, the stench of the

rawhide in his nostrils and the picture of the swarming ants torturing his mind, Jordan fought the grim spectre of despair. Bound and gagged, clasped in the ever-tightening grip of the shrinking hide, he fought to steel himself into acceptance of fate. But the primal urge to live, to struggle, however hopelessly, was strong. He writhed and twisted, ignoring the pain from lacerated wrists, until, his strength spent, he lay inert, half-choked by the gag, chest heaving as he fought for breath.

As he lay lax, the musical tinkle of Cold Creek reached his ears. Every nerve tautened as inspiration seized him.

Again he began to heave, throwing his weight from side to side, rocking the unwieldy bulk of the cowhide in which he was swathed. Finally, he succeeded in rolling over, and lay on his side, facing the direction of the creek. With concentrated attention, he examined the terrain that lay between him and the creek bank, perhaps twenty paces distant. One small rise would doom the plan that had bloomed in his brain.

But Lady Luck chose to smile. The ground sloped downhill and, moreover, was free of growth except for heat-shrunk tufts of grass. Along the creek, chaparral clustered thick, except in one spot where it had been hacked away to allow crossing from the barn.

With renewed hope, he began to rock again. But sway his body as hard as he would he could not roll the loose-wrapt, sagging bundle of hide. It cushioned the ground. Finally, the sweating, straining prisoner was compelled to quit from sheer exhaustion. Then his spine prickled at the feel of ants, pouring over the loose neckband of his shirt and spreading over the back of his neck. He went berserk, flailing and threshing like a madman.

The hairy hulk of the hide shook and quivered before the crazed ferocity of his efforts. He began to roll, slowly, clumsily, the soggy bundle gaining impetus as he redoubled his efforts to impel it. As best he could, he steered for the gap in the chaparral that marked the creek crossing. The thought entered his mind that when the ungainly roll hit the steep slope down to the water it would accelerate its speed beyond control and he would probably drown when it plunked into the creek. At least, he decided, that would be a quick and merciful death.

But the clumsy roll came to an abrupt stop at the top of the sandy incline that slanted down to the creek. It was jammed by the brush. The cleared space was not wide enough to allow passage. Branches whipped Jordan's face. He wrenched and strained, felt the lower end of the roll slide downward. Then, angled catty-corner, it again came to a stop, the top snagged by low brush. He raised his head and peered through a tangle of twigs.

Below him flowed the creek. Perhaps ten

feet wide at this point and almost waist deep, it foamed and gurgled over a bouldery bed. If he had continued to roll down that steep slope, he reflected, all the luck in the world wouldn't have saved him from drowning. With renewed hope, he figured his chances. If he could slide down, feet first, there was a gambling chance he could stop the roll before it plunged into the creek. Jerking his body, he wrenched free of the brush.

Dust rose as the cumbersome roll began slowly skidding down the slope. It came to a stop where the ground levelled on the very brink of the surging water. Again, the prisoner flailed his body from side to side, angled his clumsy burden, heaved it over and over, each turn rolling it deeper and deeper into the water. Triumph flooded him as he felt a wet chill seeping up to his knees. Thrashing like a maniac to keep the roll in motion, he was rewarded by a dampness that soaked up to his thighs. The current began to take a hand. He was conscious of a lightening of the load, an easing of the effort required to turn over.

Almost too late, he realized the danger of being swept completely off the bank. Spreading his elbows, he threw his weight backward. The motion slowed, stopped. As the hide became permeated with water he felt its soggy weight sinking. When it settled, he cautiously raised his head.

From his shoulders down he was under

water. The current surged against the roll, but it was securely wedged among mossy boulders. The chill of the creek bit through to the very marrow of his bones. But that chill was solace to his soul. A hide hardened and shrank as it dried; softened and stretched when it was immersed in water. Well content, he lay and gratefully soaked.

After a while, he began to test the rawhide thong that cut into his wrists. Unlike the hide, the leather was old and dried out. Patiently, he locked fingers behind his back, strained and pulled against the lashing, striving to stretch it. The rawhide cut still further into the flesh, but the chill of Cold Creek numbed his limbs and deadened the pain. At last, wrenching, he slipped a hand free. With a flood of exhilaration, he brought his arms to the front. Levering with his elbows he began to wriggle out inch by inch, from the clinging weight of the water-soaked hide.

Finally he stood upright in yielding mud, free of his soggy prison. He slipped the bandana off his mouth and breathed deeply, tingling with elation. He felt as though he had been delivered from the tomb, and a tomb it would have been, he thought soberly, before sundown. With disgust, he kicked the bunched hide out into the current, watching it float away.

Then he lifted his .45 out of the sodden holster and wryly watched water drip from it.

He had to clean and dry that gun fast.

Thought of Chumbley's body, lying in the grave, entered his mind. He trudged up the sandy slope to the bank top. The bulk of the barn lay between him and the cabin, a welcome screen.

The Englishman lay where he had dropped; flies formed a droning cloud around the blood caked upon his shirt. Jordan yanked the shirt up, ripped off a strip, inadvertently touching Chumbley's soft white belly. He recoiled as though he had been stung—the flesh was warm!

Scarcely believing that there still could be life in the man, he tore the shirt open and examined the wound. Clotted blood had sealed a small puckered hole in Chumbley's chest. The wondering Jordan fingered a wrist and detected a feeble pulse beat. He dropped the slack arm and straightened, eying the prone form with creased brow. Here was a new factor, he had a badly wounded man on his hands.

Chances were that Chumbley would never survive the long, jolting ride to town, he mused, weakened as the man was by loss of blood and with a slug in the chest. Yet he couldn't be left here to die. There was Irish, too. Lengthening shadows warned that sundown was creeping closer. The breed was liable to make an appearance any moment.

First things first, considered Jordan soberly.

If his luck failed to hold he was liable to join Chumbley in that grave before the sun set. He hunkered against the side of the grave, lifted out his Colt, pressed the release key under the gun, and dropped the heavy cylinder onto a palm. He shook out five shells, one spent. Setting the four loads in the sun, he got busy with the dry strip off Chumbley's shirt, wiping and drying.

From the cover of the chaparral along the creek, he eyed the cabin. Irish's tall form was sprawled on the bench outside. The breed's pony, with the dun, drifted around the pole corral nearby. Shadows of the scrub oak on the flat reached far across the sun-cured grass and the western sky was flooded with scarlet glory as the sun dropped behind the San Marcos. Jordan, still edgy from his ordeal in the slow-shrinking hide, had a fancy the sky was washed with blood.

As he watched, the tall man in front of the cabin rose and stretched lazily. In no haste, he picked up his Spencer, hooked it by the sling over a shoulder, and headed for the creek with long, swinging strides. His fiery red hair glinted in the lingering light.

Crouched in the brush, Jordan heard the breed splash across creek. Peering, he saw Irish check abruptly, head swerving as he searched the ground, one hand loosely grasping the rifle sling. Behind him, Jordan stepped out of concealment and edged closer.

He had approached to within a dozen paces when the breed swung around, at the same time slipping the Spencer free of his shoulder.

Levelling his .45, Jordan stood facing him. For once the rider noted emotion in the hard, blue eyes—a startled inredulity.

'Back a pace or so,' barked Jordan. 'Then you'll drop into the grave when I plug you. I wouldn't want to lay a hand on your rotten carcass.' He eased closer.

As fast and as ferociously as a cornered cougar, Irish blurred into action. Simultaneously, he hurled the rifle and leaped, long arms outstretched, fingers hooked, flinging himself at the shorter man.

The .45 roared, roared again as Jordan ducked to one side and loosed another slug. The breed shrieked. His long form hit the ground with a flat thud. With no compunction, Jordan watched the long form whip around, spasmodically writhing, arms and legs flailing, like a mortally wounded sidewinder.

Wary, the rider watched the threshing slowly lessen as life sceped out of the breed, until he lay slack and still, hooked fingers dug into the earth.

Indifferently, Jordan turned over the body with a boot toe, ripped off the breed's bandana and flaming red shirt. The bandana he washed in the creek and carefully wrung out. Returning to the grave, he jumped down and felt Chumbley's pulse again. It seemed stronger. He wadded the damp bandana and placed it over the bullet hole, tore up the red shirt for bandaging. Then he raised the limp form and eased it across a shoulder, climbed out of the excavation and packed his burden to the barn.

This done, he trudged back to the breed. He felt weary, bone-weary. 'I should leave the skunk for the buzzards,' he muttered, then, with a resigned lift of the shoulders, grabbed the two outstretched legs, hauled the lifeless form to the grave and toppled it in. Slowly, laboriously, he shovelled in sufficient earth to cover it.

Lassitude now seemed to lead every limb. He dragged himself back to the barn and stood eying Chumbley's form. Eyes closed, limbs slack, the man might have been dead except for that flicker of pulse.

What to do? Jordan strove to force his numbed brain into coherent thought. His head felt as though it had been split with an axe and his body as if it had been trampled by a horse. He fought an urge to just flop down and rest. But he knew that once down, Chumbley would likely be dead before he summoned the energy to get up again.

Fingering the bump on the back of his head, he strove to make a logical decision. If he tried to pack the wounded man to Clearwater on Irish's calico, odds were the ride would kill the Englishman, and he doubted if he could sit a saddle that far himself. In a flash, the solution came—Razorback's place, up creek. Maybe Carol would be home; she would know what to do. He flogged his tired brain, trying to remember if this was a week-end. She had said she spent week-ends with her brother, but he just couldn't figure what day it was.

Razorback's place was a low, long, three-room cabin set in a fenced meadow, through which Cold Creek curled. Apart, stood a network of pens and hog houses. Actually, it lay a scant three miles up creek. To the overspent Jordan, nerves ragged and body flabby as a wet sack, the ride seemed unending.

Sagging in the saddle, leading the calico, upon which he had roped Chumbley, he pulled up to the cabin in the gloom of approaching night. Carol Hall, busy correcting school papers inside, heard the clatter of hooves and rose with quick surprise. Visitors in this part of the valley were few. Opening the door, she stood eyeing with amazement what was apparently a dead man lying across a pony's withers and Jordan's drooping form.

'Why, Bill,' she cried. 'Whatever happened?'

Listlessly he slipped to the ground and indicated Chumbley. 'Shot,' he said hoarsely, 'in the chest. Better get a sawbones.' Swaying, he grabbed the saddlehorn for support.

'You're half-dead yourself,' exclaimed the

143

girl. Raising her voice, she cried, 'Jack, come quick!'

A chunky, square-featured young fellow, wearing bib overalls, stepped around the angle of the cabin. At the girl's urgent gesture, he dropped the bucket he was carrying and hastened forward.

'That man's badly wounded,' said the girl, indicating Chumbley, 'and this is Bill Jordan, our neighbor. He's about to drop, too.'

Jordan listened numbly. All strength seemed to have drained out of him and his head was an aching void. But he was alert enough to be thankful that Jack Hall was a man of action, and sparing with words. Without comment, the homesteader loosened the rope that held Chumbley and packed the helpless form inside. Jordan made no attempt to move. He was scared that if he loosened his grip on the horn he'd collapse. Carol slipped an arm around him. 'Come along,' she said gently. 'Jack will see to the horses.'

He suffered himself to be half led, half supported through the doorway. He remembered sinking onto a couch and blinking at a glass-bowled lamp set on a polished oval table; Carol yanking off his boots and lifting his legs onto the couch. Then he sank into the deep sleep of exhaustion.

CHAPTER FOURTEEN

When Jordan awakened, he stared around in bewilderment, trying to figure out why he was lying upon a leather-upholstered couch, with a soft pillow beneath his head. The floor was planked, and neatly swept. Gilt-framed pictures decorated the walls, and a treadle sewing machine stood in a corner. On an oval table sat a slim vase, holding colorful blooms.

Recollection flowed back—the treachery of Irish, the wet hide, Chumbley's shooting, a wearisome trip through gathering darkness, and—most distinctly of all—remembrance of Carol's clear tones. So he had reached Razorback's place!

He swung his legs to the floor and pulled on his boots. Behind the couch, a drawn shade glowed golden. He reached, raised the shade and slitted his eyes against sunglare. Close upon noon, he registered, he had slept the clock around.

A pot rattled behind a closed rear door and there were sounds of movement. When he turned the knob, he found himself in a lean-to kitchen. And, busy at a stove, was Carol Hall, wearing a crisp cotton house dress.

'Guess I woke up in Paradise, among the angels,' he drawled.

The girl turned with a smile. 'And I guess

145

you feel a lot better than you did last night.'

'Fit enough to fight a fistful of wildcats,' he grinned. His tone changed, 'How's Chumbley doing?'

She slid a pie into the oven. 'The wounded man? Scarcely alive.' Her voice was sober. 'You didn't—' she hesitated, fishing for words.

'Nope, I didn't plug the Limey. I shoulda packed him to town, but I just didn't figure he'd make it—me neither.'

'Jack left for Clearwater last night,' she told him. 'He should be back before dark with Doctor Harley. I do hope they will not be too late.' She glanced curiously at his red-wealed wrists, 'Just what is it all about?'

He shrugged. 'It's a long story.'

'Well,' she directed briskly, 'sit down and relate it. I'll pour a cup of coffee and serve a late breakfast. No story—no breakfast!'

As she bustled around, he related the events of the previous day, from the discovery of the telescope to the breed's burial. When he was through, Carol commented thoughtfully, 'I should have warned you against that half-breed. Folks claim Leggett and Negg would never have evaded the law, if he hadn't led them to a hide-away in the Barrens, and packed in supplies.'

'Wal, the gent's troubles are all over now,' returned Jordan philosophically, and devoted himself to the agreeable task of demolishing a sizzling plateful of bacon and eggs, with fried

146

potatoes on the side.

'I suppose,' persisted Carol, 'that you will continue to search for the loot?"

'Could be!' he admitted offhand.

'And you'll turn it over to Sheriff Haslipp?'

'Who else?' he countered blandly.

She darted a sharp glance in his direction, but made no reply.

After he had eaten, the girl conducted him to a bedroom. Between white sheets on a shiny brass bedstead lay Chumbley. The Englishman's once ruddy features were shrunken and gray. He breathed laboriously, and there was crimson froth upon his lips.

'His lungs!' explained Carol worriedly. 'There's really nothing I can do.' Jordan mentally decided there was little anyone could do and he wouldn't wager a beer check on Chumbley's chance of pulling through. Then he gave thought to a more pleasant subject— the prospect of a whole lazy day spent in Carol's company.

Disillusionment came quickly. He was the only able-bodied man on the place and there were plenty chores to be handled. There was a cow to be milked, hogs to be fed, water to be pumped, feed to be mixed, horses to be tended. When he finally found time to relax, Razorback and a graying man, wearing a creased store suit, rode in. A black bag suspended from the saddlehorn of the townsman's plump gelding marked him as the doctor. Attention focussed on the wounded man. When the doctor announced his intention of staying over, Jordan decided he'd head back to his own cabin.

Darkness wreathed the river when he jogged up to the pole corral and stripped the gear off his mount. Outside the silent cabin he paused, his glance sweeping the shadowed flat. He fought an intangible feeling of menace and laid it to ragged nerves. The dun seemed restless, too, drifting around the corral.

Then, like a winking red eye, a gunshot flashed from the dark wall of brush along the creek. Another, and another followed, shattering the quiet and rumbling away into distance. Lead snicked into the ground and punched into the timbers of the cabin, With the first shot, Jordan whirled and dove for the doorway. Inside, he hastily slammed the door and set the bar in place. Handicapped by darkness, he groped around, found the Winchester and levered a shell into the breach. Crouched, he listened to a leaden blast, as guns around the cabin spilled flame and thunder, and lead droned through the shattered windows or flattened against the walls.

Brow creased, he considered the sudden attack. The volume of fire banished all doubt as to the identity of his attackers. It was the Turtle bunch, back to finish the job the sheriff's posse had interrupted.

Not much chance of a sheriff's posse this time, he thought somberly. No posse from Clearwater could reach him before dawn, and he'd likely be buzzard bait before the sun rose again.

Snatching a quick glance through a window frame, he could see nothing beyond spurts of fire, blooming like red roses against the night. They didn't seem to be pushing too hard, he reflected.

He didn't know that Buck Burdock, who nursed a hate like an Indian, had posted riders in the hills to watch the sheriff's lookout. When the deputy had pulled out to report strange doings at Harker's place—a gunshot behind the barn and the wanton killing and skinning of a Turtle steer—word had sped to the Turtle. This time, Burdock was assured he could clean up on the stubborn new owner of Harker's without interference.

Tempo of the gunfire began to speed up. Hunkered by the stove, nursing the Winchester, Jordan decided he would be wasting ammunition if he replied to the fire. If the Turtle hands figured him dead, and ventured closer, then opportunity would arise for retaliation.

He sniffed, suddenly taut. Wood smoke tainted the air. The crackle of dry brush, afire, reached his ears. Jumping to his feet, he quested around the cabin, peering out, seeking to locate the fire. His search was quickly over.

Through chinks between the logs, behind the bunk, a red glare was plain. Distracting his attention with gunfire, the attackers had heaped brush against the end of the cabin and set it ablaze.

Crackling grew louder as the flames took hold. Smoke began to filter between the timbers, and as the smoke thickened, the heat grew. Jordan stood weighing his predicament. He had to get out fast, before the growing glare from the fire lit up the terrain around the cabin and made him a plain mark. The Turtle bunch knew that if he didn't duck out, he'd soon smother, or roast. Chances were, they were watching that door like hawks.

Smoke fouled the air now, irritating his eyes and rasping his throat. He dropped flat on the floor, and found breathing a mite easier. Crawling to the doorway, he reached up and knocked the bar down. Flinging open the door, he flattened.

As he expected, the night was pinpointed with orange stabs of flame and a hail of lead droned through the doorway.

He wormed across the dirt floor, toward the rear window. Here he came quickly to his feet, knocked out remaining fragments of glass with the barrel of his Winchester, tossed the gun aside and began to wriggle through the aperture. His shoulders made a tight fit and he ripped his shirt into shreds, but he made it. Head foremost, he dropped to the ground, crawled along the cabin, rounded a corner and lay in the shadow. Rifles still whipcracked as the Turtle bunch threw lead through the open doorway. Burdock would have one heck of a cartridge bill to foot, considered the fugitive with ironic amusement.

The flickering reflection of the fire at the further end of the cabin threw grotesque shadows writhing across the ground.

On hands and knees, he began to crawl away, heading for the creek. An excited yell told him he had been sighted. Lead began to splatter around. He jumped to his feet and made a run for it, racing for the dark wall of chaparral that marked the creek bank, zig-zagging like a startled jackrabbit.

Like a wolf pack giving voice at prospect of the kill, yelling punchers were converging from all sides. Sucking air into his laboring lungs, the harried Jordan bounded over low brush, thankful that cottony clouds billowed over the moon, giving his pursuers no more than a fleeting shadow for a mark.

Gasping, he slackened and snatched a quick glance behind. The cabin now blazed fiercely, tongues of flame licking high above its roof. Silhouetted by the fire, the forms of men were distinct, all laboring in his direction, and as much handicapped by high-heeled riding boots as he was.

A renewed outburst of yelling, the zip of lead, told him that he had been sighted again and this was no time for delay.

Again darting and dodging, he sped off. The clumped chaparral of the creek loomed close now. A few more panting steps and he plunged into thick brush. Bent arms protecting his face, he bulled through a mat of threshing branches and whipping twigs. Then, abruptly, the ground seemed to fall away beneath his feet. He plunged down, down, down, gasped as his body broke the surface of the creek with a resounding splash and icy-cold water drenched him; he choked as he went under.

Spluttering and gasping, he found his feet and floundered around, jostled by the fast-running current. Fingering blindly, in the gloom, he fastened onto a protruding root that jutted from the bank, and steadied. Feeling like a half-drowned puppy, he stood fighting for breath. His shirt made a cold poultice against his body and the chill bit into his submerged legs. It was too dark to see anything, beyond the steep banks rising like walls on either side. The sound of breaking brush was plain as pursuers quested around, hunting his trail.

He had to keep moving, decided the fugitive. Before sun-up they'd beat every square foot of brush and would sure flush him out of the creek. Slowly, groping his way, slipping and sliding on smooth, slimy boulders, he began to work upstream. At spots, where the creek narrowed, the force of the current almost swept him off his feet. Once, he froze, scarce daring to breathe, when a puncher's form loomed on the bank overhead.

Then his luck changed. Close to full, the moon sailed serenely from behind the blanketing clouds, and laid a silver sheen on the rippling water. Struggling slowly and painfully against the current, cutbanks reaching high above on either side, the fugitive groaned. He would be a sitting duck now.

CHAPTER FIFTEEN

Plain in the moonlight, leaning against the pull of the current, the fugitive checked. Nearby, he could hear his pursuers smashing through brush. At any moment one might appear on either bank and glance down—and that would be the end of Bill Jordan. To steady himself, he reached out and grasped a knotted root projecting from the crumbling bank. Above him towered a storm-blasted old cottonwood. Through the years the lapping waters of the creek had eroded away the sandy earth of the bank below it, exposing a tangle of gnarled roots. In the moonlight, they reminded Jordan of a writhing octopus, wreathed in a curtain of dangling vines that dangled from the bank above.

Crashing in the brush drew closer now, and it was apparent that someone was pushing through the chaparral toward the creek. This was the finish, thought the fugitive. He was stuck in the creek like a fly in a glue-pot, with no place to hide. To prolong inevitable discovery, he waded close to the bank and pressed against the curtain of greenery that festooned the jumble of roots. To his surprise, it yielded. He thrust through, and stood knee-deep in water in what was apparently a shallow cave, undercut by the current during some flash flood. Behind him, the matted vines swung back, effectually concealing his unexpected hideaway.

Through the remainder of the night, chilled, with chattering teeth, he stood in water, clinging to the twisted roots of the cottonwood for support, listening to the sounds of the relentless manhunt around him—the shouts of men, crackling of brush, once the roar of a gun. In the obscurity he could see nothing.

Gradually, as dawn approached and the gloom around became tinged with gray, sound of pursuit died. With growing light, a tracery of trailing vine not a foot from his face was revealed. He moved stiff limbs. Feet and legs had long lost all feeling from immersion in the chilly creek. His garb hung wet and cold upon him. He peered around, seeking opportunity to hoist himself out of the numbing water. Then he saw that the sandy floor of the rude cave sloped upward beneath a tangle of huge roots, its recesses cloaked in obscurity. Thankfully, he hauled himself out of the stream, ducking and squirming between the roots. His right knee collided with a sharp object and he repressed a quick 'Ouch!'

Glancing down, he saw that he had struck the corner of a box, half-concealed in loose earth. Curious, he bent and hauled it out with both hands. It was roped. He dug into a pants pocket and brought out a damp jackknife, sliced the rope, raised the box lid—and froze with the shock of discovery. To the brim the box was filled with neat packages of greenbacks, unsoiled currency, fresh from the mint. He grabbed a wad of twenty-dollar bills and eyed it with fast-beating pulse. By sheer fool luck, he had stumbled over Jed Harker's cache.

But there was no quarter-million in that box, he reflected. Dropping the wad of greenbacks back into the box and closing the lid, he began digging into the earth with the jackknife, shoveling the loose fragments away with his free hand. His fingers came in contact with the rough texture of a gunnysack. Redoubling his efforts, he uncovered it, grabbed with both hands and yanked. It was bulging, heavy and hard. Cutting away a thong that secured the neck, he dipped into it and came out with a fat buckskin pouch. It clinked. Heart fast beating, he opened up the pouch, tilted it.

A glittering stream of double-eagles spilled out. Scarcely believing that it was not all a dream, he fingered the gold, then, with growing elation, gathered the yellow coins scattered over the earth between his feet and dropped them into a pants pocket.

Finally, he had found the treasure that had drawn him up from the Rio Grande. Here was wealth beyond his most sanguine dreams. But would he survive to enjoy the fruits of his gamble?

156

For the balance of the day he lay concealed in the shallow cave, trying to ignore the complaint of a shrinking paunch and an occasional shout that told his pursuers had not yet abandoned the hunt. Luckily, he considered, none had the hardihood to wade up creek and examine the banks. But who would dream of a cave? What quirk of fate had revealed its existence to Jed Harker?

As he hunkered in the fading light of another dying day, he gave thought to his next move. It was a sure thing he couldn't cower in that cave indefinitely. Hunger, at least, would drive him out. But he had to outwait Buck Burdock and his crew. When the Turtle bunch quit searching and pulled out, he'd hit for Irish's place and grab a pack pony and a saddle horse, too, if Burdock had grabbed his dun. Then, unmolested, he would load the loot and be shut of Harker's—for keeps.

Quiet settled on the creek, except for the faint murmuring of its swirling waters, and the fugitive could restrain himself no longer. Cautiously, he wormed through the curtain of vines.

The pesky moon again rode high, casting a pale sheen over brush and creek. The tangled roots of the cottonwood offered plenty handholds and made his climb to the top of the steep cutbank an easy matter. Beside the massive trunk he stood unmoving, ears alert for sound of movement. All seemed quiet.

Wary as a lobo, he began to ease through the brush.

A pony whinnied somewhere ahead, and another answered. The fugitive checked. So there were still riders hanging around. Again he ghosted forward.

Finally, screened by the brush, he stared across the shadow-pitted flat at a dark blotch that marked the site of his cabin. Nothing remained now, except the squat, smoke-blackened square of the stove, protruding from heaped embers like an ulcerated tooth.

Questing in the direction of barn and corral, he focused a camp fire, glowing like a huge cigarette butt, in front of the barn. Hunkered around it were four punchers. Close by, a rider was restlessly pacing. He recognized Buck Burdock's burly form.

That Burdock *hombre* was more persistent than a hell-fly, reflected the fugitive. As long as he stuck around with his riders there'd be no chance of removing the loot. And how long could Jordan afford to wait? Right then he was hungry enough to eat a saddle blanket, and the nearest source of food was Razorback's place. Odds were that Burdock had it covered. He daren't shoot game, the sound of a shot would bring the Turtle crew buzzing around like hornets.

A dry stick crackled behind him. He whirled and glimpsed the dim outline of a man. In a flash, he flung himself at the intruder, reaching

158

for his throat in a desperate attempt to choke off a yell of alarm.

Two muscular arms wrapped around him and he thought his ribs would crack as their pressure tightened. Fingers thrusting through thick beard, he groped for his opponent's throat.

Interlocked, the pair went down, rolling and grunting. He heard an agonized gasp as he rammed a knee into the other's groin. Then he was flying through the air as the bearded man flung him off. He came down on his back, with a jolt that drove the air from his lungs and left him, momentarily, gasping and impotent. Before he could move, his opponent's solid bulk-plunked down on his chest and iron fingers fastened upon his windpipe. 'Brother,' came Paul's deep tones, 'you are due to shake hands with St. Peter.'

'The Preacher!' croaked Jordan. 'I quit!'

'Well, well!' murmured Paul, his grip slackening. 'So it's that fiery young stallion the Turtle is hellbound to round up.' He removed his weight from the fugitive's chest.

Jordan sat up, tenderly fingering his throat. 'You sure play rough,' he grumbled.

'You, brother,' smiled Paul, 'were in no amiable mood.'

'Would you be if a pack of wolves burned you out and hunted you down like a coyote?' demanded Jordan irately.

'Love ye your enemies and you shall surely

find your reward in Paradise,' reproved the Preacher sonorously.

'If I can get rid of said enemies I ain't worrying about the reward,' retorted Jordan.

The Preacher eyed him keenly, hunkered, then picked something carelessly off the ground.

'Veritably Burdock is an oppressor,' he intoned. 'And he mocks the Word. Such shall surely feed the fires of Hell.'

'Say,' the fugitive told him earnestly, 'I just got to get them *hombres* out of here.'

The Preacher smiled, his attention elsewhere as he plucked here and there in the dry grass. 'Is the matter so very urgent?' he inquired.

'It's my land!' threw back Jordan, and then realized how lame the excuse must sound.

'But for Burdock,' murmured the other, stroking his beard, 'you would be unmolested. His hatred of opposition is a canker, eating into his soul. To the crew, the matter is a chore, a chore they do not relish, for they do not stomach your sting.'

'But for Burdock they'd quit?'

'As surely as night follows day.'

The fugitive considered this awhile. 'If I could just brace Burdock, man to man,' he muttered.

The Preacher tugged at his beard, deep in thought. Then he intoned, "Thou shalt not kill, saith the Lord. But the Good Book also

160

reminds us that there is a time to kill.' Abruptly, his tone changed to the conversational, 'It shall be arranged! They tolerate me, respecting the Cloth. Injun close to the camp fire. When I step up to the punchers, you brace Burdock.' He brought out his gun, twirled the cylinder.

Jordan jumped eagerly to his feet. 'Afore I pull out,' he begged, 'give me five shells. Mine been watersoaked so much I'm scared of a misfire.'

Without comment, the Preacher slipped the shells from the loops in his gunbelt and dropped them into the rider's palm.

The light in the bearded man's eyes was akin to amusement as he watched Jordan ghost away through the brush.

Sliding from one patch of shadow to another, the fugitive worked closer and closer to the group by the fire. Chewing cigarettes, the four hunkered punchers traded low-voiced talk. Burdock's bull-necked form was plain as he stood close by, scowling into the night.

The punchers' heads jerked around as Paul's rawboned form loomed in the flickering circle of light. The Preacher came to a stop across the fire from the punchers and boomed a greeting to Burdock. The cowman abruptly turned his back and moved off a few paces.

Too close now for further concealment, Jordan straightened and began to walk openly toward the camp fire. If Paul failed him, he thought, he'd likely to be a sieve in less than two minutes.

A smothered oath from one of the punchers told that he had been sighted. The man braced to jump to his feet, when Paul whipped out his .45. His deep voice boomed, 'Freeze, brethren! One move and you jump plumb into Hell.'

Four pairs of startled eyes dwelt on the steel barrel of a levelled Colt. Four men remained motionless.

Burdock spun around, roared as he glimpsed Jordan advancing and grabbed for his gun. It was out when the fugitive's slug took him, high and center. He staggered. With desperate effort he levered up his sagging gun-arm and thumbed. The bullet plowed ground. The gun spilled from his relaxed fingers. He dropped with a heavy thud, so heavily that the ground seemed to shake, and lay unmoving.

Jordan restored his smoking gun to the holster and spun around to face the slack-jawed punchers. 'Any of you gents care to take it up?' he inquired.

The challenge was received with tight silence.

'Then beat it!' he barked. 'You're trespassing and I reckon you know it. Get off my land!'

For seconds the Turtle riders remained still, bewildered by the surge of events. Then one rose, and the others followed suit. In a knot they headed for the corral.

The Preacher holstered his gun. 'The Lord shall destroy the wicked,' he intoned, 'but for those who believe there is everlasting life.'

'Who craves to live forever?' growled Jordan. 'You got the makin's?'

The two watched the Turtle hands saddle up and jog away into the night. 'You lamp more of Burdock's boys around?' inquired Jordan, fashioning a smoke.

'No, brother,' Paul assured him. 'All but those four were ordered back to the ranch. Burdock is a cowman at heart, he knows there is always work to be done on the range.'

'You sure don't miss much,' commented the rider thoughtfully.

'Not even the gold you so carelessly scatter,' returned the Preacher urbanely. He dug into the tails of his frock coat, tossed a shining gold coin to the astounded Jordan. More followed, in shimmering sequence.

'There are more where we wrestled in the brush, brother,' said Paul. 'You shed double-eagles like a dog sheds fleas.'

CHAPTER SIXTEEN

Jordan concealed his chagrin as he caught the spinning coins. 'Guess my money belt broke,' he said quickly, too quickly. 'Been packing that dinero around for a coon's age.'

Then he could have bitten off his tongue. Even by firelight, it was plain the gold was newly-minted.

But Paul seemed uninterested. He kicked more fuel onto the fire, and hunkered, holding his hands to the blaze, for there was a bite to the night air. 'You'll rebuild the cabin, brother?' he inquired idly.

Jordan dropped down across the fire. 'Nope,' he declared. 'I'm quitting. Had a bellyful of Harker's place. The spread's brought me nothing but grief. Reckon I'll make tracks for my old stamping ground, the Rio Grande.'

'And cease to set your heart upon riches?' Jordan thought he detected an undertone of mockery in the Preacher's deep voice, but the other met his glance with bland complacency. 'If you got Harker's cache in mind,' he grunted, 'forget it. It's a pipe dream.'

'He that seeketh earthly riches, seeketh dross,' intoned the other. 'The wise man lays up treasure in Heaven. I rejoice, brother, that you have achieved wisdom.'

When the fire guttered down to reddening ashes, Jordan yawned, strolled across to the corral and came back with his rolled up slicker. He wrapped up in it and stretched out. The Preacher stalked out into the darkness, as was his habit, to bed down alone.

With sunup, he had vanished. Glad to be alone, Jordan shot a couple of rabbits, grilled them and then gave thought to his next move. There seemed to be no more obstacles to cleaning out the cache.

He saddled the dun and hit for Irish's place, now deserted, except for a handful of ponies drifting around a large fenced pasture. He roped a sturdy roan, cinched on one of several old packsaddles that lay behind the breed's shack, and adjusted a macarty. Then he headed back to Harker's place, leading the pack animal.

It seemed at last he was to be left in peace, considered the rider, as he crossed the creek and rounded the barn. A sprinkling of Turtle stock had found its way around the wire fence and grazed across the flat. But he had more urgent things on his mind than Turtle cows.

Following the creek, he checked at the storm-battered cottonwood and stepped out of leather. Tying the two ponies, he stood, surveying the brush around, senses acute, soaking in the peace and quiet. It just didn't seem possible, he reflected, that after all the scheming and shooting that had marked his

165

brief sojourn on Cold Creek, his quest was to end so simply and easily as this.

He climbed down the bank, clinging to the twisted roots of the cottonwood and, standing knee-deep in water, parted the screen of vines. When he stepped into the rude cave, the abrupt transition from sunglare to dim obscurity blinded him. For no reason, panic flooded him. Maybe some puncher had kept cases on his movements and cleaned the cache out. Then his vision cleared. Relief flooded him as he focused the box, a bulging gunnysack beside it, set on the loose earth. Thirty minutes later he yanked a canvas over the pack pony's load, secured it firmly with a diamond hitch, bent to tighten the cinches of the roan when sound of a familiar voice straightened him. He pivoted—to stare into the muzzle of Paul's .45, held in a firm hand.

'All gold is dross?' intoned the Preacher, lurking devilment in his piercing eyes. 'This, brother, is for the good of your soul.' His tone sharpened, 'Unbuckle the gunbelt, Jordan— and no shenanigans. Buck and you'll join Burdock in hell.'

Tight-lipped, Jordan loosened the buckle and his gunbelt dropped. Then he ejaculated, with bitter venom, 'You double-crossing son of a bitch!'

Paul's white teeth flashed in an amused smile. 'Put not your trust in princes, brother, nor in mortal man. The flesh, alas, is weak.

Now back a mite!'

His victim reluctantly stepped backward.

The Preacher hooked the gunbelt with a boot toe and swung it into the creek. 'Had you cut me in, brother,' he told the fuming rider regretfully, 'you would have shared in the spoils. Saith the Good Book, he that is greedy of gain shall lose all.'

Still covering Jordan, he swung into the dun's saddle, the tails of his rusty frock coat trailing. '*Adios!*' he cried, raising the reins. 'I have a long and weary ride ahead, through the Barrens.'

'So you're a hoss thief, too!' gritted Jordan.

'I will loose the dun, when I am beyond pursuit,' smiled Paul. 'He will drift back to the river. The Lord loveth a prudent man!'

He pushed his frock coat back, slipped the gun into leather and grabbed the dangling lead rope of the pack pony. Jordan watched as the two animals cantered briskly out of sight along the creek bank. Then, with a resigned shrug, he began to climb down the creek bank, to retrieve his gunbelt.

*   *   *

Clearwater drowsed in the torrid heat of midday, when a rider jogged down Main Street, a laden pack pony in the lead. Outside the narrow-windowed courthouse he wheeled to the rail, stepped down and looped the reins of the buckskin he rode around the hitch rail. A good chunk of horse-flesh, he reflected, but he'd be glad to get the dun back.

When he jingled into the law office, the sheriff swung massively around in his swivel chair, chewing a cold cigar. 'Wal,' he rumbled, 'if it's not Mister Trouble himself. What shenanigans you been up to out at Cold Creek? Carol Hall reported you brought in the Limey. The gent's perking up, claims Irish shot him.'

'And I shot Irish!' replied Jordan laconically. 'There never was a clearer case of self-defense.' He dropped onto a chair, and added coolly, 'Beefed Buck Burdock, too!'

'You—killed—Buck!' Haslipp almost lost the composure he had cultivated through long years of interrogating law-breakers. Mentally, a vision of the cattlemen's vote disappearing down the drain, was ghastly torture.

'Yep!' admitted his visitor, with no embarrassment. 'The big buffalo set a torch to my cabin. I braced him. He drew first. I got four witnesses—Turtle punchers.' As the sheriff assimilated this, he added, 'I'm quitting Harker's place!'

There, thought Haslipp numbly, went his sole hope for re-election and the recovery of the loot from the train hold-up. He had been banking on this lean gun-wolf from the Rio Grande to lead him to it. Another busted flush.

Tonelessly, he returned, 'What do you

crave—congratulations?'

'Yep,' smiled Jordan, 'I located the loot.'

'You what?' The sheriff's cigar dropped from his lips. He stared unbelievingly at his visitor.

'Packed it to town,' volunteered Jordan. 'It's outside, right now.'

Haslipp shot to his feet as though impelled by a powder charge and cycloned for the door. The rider tailing him, he moved down the corridor at a run and practically bounced down the courthouse steps. While Jordan stood by, amused, he began feverishly to loosen the rope that bound the load to the pack pony. 'If you're hurrahin' me, Jordan,' he promised hoarsely, 'I'll shoot you, so help me.'

Five minutes later the sheriff was beaming as he feasted his eyes upon stacked wads of greenbacks and a pile of buckskin pouches, heavy with gold, heaped upon his desk. Jordan was casually looking over the 'Wanted' notices that plastered the wall. He paused before one, brought out a stub of pencil and began idly sketching in a beard.

Haslipp turned, all geniality now. 'Reckon you got a thumping big bounty coming—fifty thousand cartwheels, I'd say.'

'I figured thataway,' returned Jordan nonchalantly. 'Guess I'll resign, now I'm in clover.'

'Resign?' The sheriff stared.

'Texas Rangers! Was assigned to undercover

work in Santa Monte. That's where I bumped into Harker—and I sure didn't stick that knife in his back.'

Haslipp shook his head as if to clear it. What next, he wondered.

'You acquainted with this gent?' inquired the rider. The sheriff stepped up beside him and eyed the 'Wanted' notice that Jordan indicated. The illustration showed a man with high forehead and piercing, deepset eyes. He had been clean-shaven before Jordan had pencilled in a bushy beard. Below, Haslipp read:

$1,000 REWARD

for apprehension of Samuel Larsen, alias Scripture Sam. Wanted for bank robbery, with violence. Height 6"2'. Age 32. Weight 220. Black hair. Hook nose. Held up Winchester County Bank, Culver City Bank, and National Bank of Pueblo. Dangerous gunman. Well educated, trained for Holy Orders. Operates alone.

G. H. Wilson, Sheriff,
Culver County, Texas.

'That wouldn't be the bearded psalm singer who's gallivanting around the Valley, forking a mule,' inquired Haslipp thoughtfully.

'I reckon it would,' drawled Jordan.

'I'll get the boys busy and round up the

170

hombre,' said the sheriff.

'Guess you're too late,' returned Jordan. 'Right now he's beating across the Barrens with a pack pony that's toting two sacks of creek sand.'

'Creek sand?' frowned Haslipp. 'The gent loco?'

'Let's just say he'll be mad enough to bite hisself when he opens up them sacks,' chuckled Jordan.

*   *   *

Hunkered against the yard fence, a lean-faced rider watched a throng of excited children erupt from the school-house. Shortly after, their teacher, Carol Hall, bonnet swinging from one hand, appeared, locked the door and headed for the gate. The rider rose to meet her.

'Why, Bill Jordan!' she exclaimed. 'Whatever are you doing in town?'

'Made a delivery, a quarter-million Chicago & Santa Fe train loot, to the sheriff,' he explained gravely.

'You found it!' she enthused. 'And turned it in! I was so afraid—' she checked, biting her lip. She spoke again, 'Now, I suppose—' for a second time she broke off.

'Don't you ever finish what you start out to say?' inquired Jordan, amusement in his eyes. 'You suppose what?"

171

'You'll be going back to where you came from,' she told him lamely.

'That depends,' he decided, after a pause.

She laughed, grasping his arm. 'Some men never finish what they start out to say,' she teased. 'Depends upon what?'

'If I accept a proposition the banker just made. Seems the bank got the Turtle on its hands. Burdock carried a heavy mortgage. I plank down ten tousand dollars and I assume the mortgage and take over the spread, lock, stock and barrel.'

'What a wonderful opportunity!'

'There's complications.'

'Complications?' She eyed him, puzzled.

'Wal, this doggoned banker craves to see a married man out there. Figures he's a better risk.'

'So?' she replied faintly, so faintly he scarcely caught the word.

'What I'm trying to work around to,' he burst out, 'is ask the prettiest gal north of the Rio Grande if she'd marry a no-good, fiddle-footed range colt.'

Her eyes were shining when she looked up at him. 'The answer is "Yes",' she replied softly, 'providing he's branded "Bill Jordan".'

The few citizens who chanced to be on Main Street gaped with wonder at the sight of a gray-shirted rider, the school ma'am wrapped in his arms, executing a frenzied war dance. She seemed to be enjoying it, too.

IOOF
WP.